The Secr

The Secret Life of Nuns

Pietro Aretino

Translated by Andrew Brown

ET REMOTISSIMA PROPE

Hesperus Classics

Hesperus Classics

Published by Hesperus Press Limited

4 Rickett Street, London SW6 1RU

www.hesperuspress.com

The Secret Life of Nuns first published in Italian as *Ragionamento, giornata prima* in 1534;

This translation first published by Hesperus Press Limited, 2004

Introduction and English language translation © Andrew Brown, 2004

Designed and typeset by Fraser Muggeridge

Printed in Italy by Graphic Studio Srl

ISBN: 1-84391-102-7

CONTENTS

You may have been to the beautiful little island of Murano, in the Venetian lagoon. Aretino, who spent most of his professional life in Venice, refers to it somewhat obliquely in *The Secret Life of Nuns*, since one thing his nuns and friars particularly enjoy is a *pastinaca muranese* – a *pastinaca* from Murano. To the innocent ear, this sounds like something you might order in a restaurant: after all, the similar word *pastina* means small pasta, or a cake. And *pastinaca* does indeed refer to something edible – a parsnip (so, in the text, I have translated it as 'parsnip from Murano'), as well as being a fish, more specifically a stingray (*Dasyatis pastinaca* or *Trygon vulgaris*). But as so often when it comes to Renaissance Italian, a better guide to the meaning of this word is John Florio, the friend of Shakespeare, who in 1611 published one of the earliest Italian-English dictionaries, which he called, with an expansive Renaissance braggadocio that would have appealed to Aretino, *Queen Anna's New World of Words*. In it, we are given some rather more enlightening information. *Pastinaca* means (I have modernised the spelling): 'a parsnip-root. Also a fork-fish or ray. Also a puffin. Also used for a man's tool. [We're getting warmer.] Also as *fagiolata*' (or *faggiolata*; his translation of this word is delightful: 'tittle tattle or flimflam talk without rhyme or reason, head or foot, as women tell when they shale peason', i.e. shell peas). But the next entry gives it away: '*pastinaca muranese*: a dildo of glass'.

And this is indeed what Aretino meant: the protagonists in what might also perhaps be called *Carry on in the Cloister* seem to be remarkably keen on resorting to glass dildoes for their sexual shenanigans – not that they give any evidence of being lousy Latin lovers, far from it; it's just that the *pastinaca muranese* adds to the range of copulatory combinations they can indulge in. ('What larks, Pippa, eh, what larks!' as Nanna might have said to her daughter: these days, they would no doubt turn up on some late-night chat show demurely discussing how unembarrassing and indeed empowering their *pastinache muranesi* have proved to be.) Murano has for centuries been famous for the quality of its glassware (in one of his letters, Aretino praises some fine goblets produced on the island – though I don't know what kind of answer you would get if you asked for a *pastinaca muranese* in one of its elegant glassware shops these days). In *The Secret Life of Nuns*, it is both a glass tool and also – as a parsnip, or, metaphorically, a sausage or a fruit – something to be eaten (and sniffed): something with which you can stuff not only your face but also other orifices. Sex, for Aretino, is one of the pleasures of life, like food and drink – and music, flowers and art, all of which slide into one another in a voluptuary's dream. Christ had given him an 'overflowing nature', he said in one of his letters, and his correspondence (much of it written to be published – as it duly was, during his own lifetime) is full of an animal vitality as well as a more delicate and subtle sensuality. Take a look at his famous portrait by Titian, his close friend. There he stands, massively present, four-square to the world, wearing the golden chain that Francis I of France had sent him: an image of power and potency – but also of the potential power of fiction, too (including the kind of teasing, fabling exaggeration we find in *The Secret Life of Nuns*), for on that gold chain were pendants of green and white, each one engraved with the words 'LINGUA EIUS LOQUETUR MENDACIUM', from Psalm 36: 30 (Vulgate), adapted to mean 'His mouth will speak lies'. Whether Francis was modestly rebuking Aretino for the flattery Aretino had heaped on him, or making an arch allusion to Aretino's falsehoods in general, is unclear: both, probably. Not that Aretino was just a flatterer: the 'Scourge of Princes', proud that his pen was mightier than their swords, could be distant or downright aggressive towards them. In 1543 the Holy Roman Emperor Charles V (another sitter for Titian) was making his way up through Italy towards the Brenner Pass, which he was to cross into Germany. Near the town of Peschiera, the Emperor spotted the Venetian delegation coming to greet him; among them was the new Duke of Urbino, accompanied by Aretino. Charles spurred on his horse and galloped forward ahead of his own men. His first question was 'Which of you is Aretino?' The writer came forward with his usual self-possession, and was invited by the Emperor to ride with him, but when Charles later invited him to come to Germany, Aretino coolly declined, saying he had decided he would never leave Venice. He frequently managed to play off one ruler against another, using both Francis and Charles, for instance, who were each other's enemies, as his patrons. But then this was a man who had the chutzpah to tell Pope Clement VII to 'turn to Christ' (after the Sack of Rome in 1527), as well as advising Michelangelo on how to paint his *Last Judgement*.

This latter episode is particularly instructive, for Aretino was both fascinated by the visual arts (a friend of Titian, as we have seen) and also, as a writer, their rival. When Michelangelo neglected to send Aretino sketches of his work in progress, Aretino took umbrage – and when he did get to see them, he claimed that he found the nudity of the figures Michelangelo was planning for the Sistine Chapel (that most sacred of Christian temples, as Aretino fulminated in a letter to the painter), quite shocking; the fresco of *The Last Judgement*, he wrote, would be worthier of a brothel than a holy choir, and

Michelangelo ought to cover over the genitals of the damned with tongues of infernal fire (and those of the blessed with sunbeams). Aware of the potential charge of hypocrisy, given his own reputation as the author of such lubricious texts as *The Secret Life of Nuns*, Aretino defended himself: I may have written about the whore Nanna, he says, but although she spoke of immodest things, she did so in a language that was decorous and comely.

It is of course amusing to read this apologia, coming as it does from the man who has been called the father of modern pornography. He has also been called the father of journalism and the father of modern art criticism, though all these honorifics are perhaps too much of a burden for any one man to bear. Giorgio Vasari – born in Arezzo like Aretino, as the latter's self-chosen surname proclaims – was a much more serious contender in the art criticism stakes. As for journalism, we can indeed speculate that, today, Aretino might well have found a niche as a media mogul, one with solid religious credentials (he produced, contemporary with *The Secret Life of Nuns*, hagiographies of the Blessed Virgin, St Catherine, and St Thomas Aquinas), but also a lucrative sideline in porn – at all events someone with enough influence for a politician to treat him with wary circumspection, if not actually to court him and his readers. However, in his stand-off with Michelangelo, Aretino was making a claim about the relative indecency of word and image. His career had always registered the tensions and complicities between the two, not least because he saw himself as striving to outdo the visual even when he was flattering the visual artists around him. A work that drew his especial attention early on in his career was the series of sixteen paintings by Giulio Romano depicting sixteen sexual postures. As usual, the latest technology (in this case, the art of engraving) soon made what would otherwise have been restricted to a small handful of *cognoscenti* available to the many, via Marcantino Raimondi's etchings. Raimondi was imprisoned by Clement VII for his pains; Aretino canvassed for his release – and composed sixteen *sonetti lussuriosi* ('Lewd Sonnets') as a kind of verbal accompaniment to the images. In *The Secret Life of Nuns*, Nanna discloses how rampant were visual representations of sex, if not actually in the cloisters, at least in Aretino's fevered imagination of them: his nuns and friars draw stimulation from paintings that sound similar to Romano's, and a present sent to Nanna, which she at first takes to be a prayer book, turns out to be more like a sex manual. In other words, Aretino includes references to the pornographic within his own pornography; there is a constant interweaving of sex with its (often visual) mimesis. This is nothing unusual: the same thing happens in Sade, where the libido of the protagonists is always being inflamed by erotic narratives and, less frequently, pictures. But again, the *need* for this supplementary stimulation (another kind of *pastinaca muranese*) is interesting: for Aretino, sex is both natural and something that needs the helping hand of art – both an instinctual, animal urge (hence the rather disagreeable story about the bitch on heat, which may have influenced an equally disagreeable passage in Rabelais's *Pantagruel*), and also a matter of artifice and refinement, in which sex needs to be constantly reinvented if it is not to be, as he puts it in a typically culinary turn of phrase, as insipid as a bean minestrone flavoured by neither salt nor olive oil. Freud commented that the sexual life of human beings is in such a permanent state of dysfunction that it is in danger of succumbing to atrophy. Aretino adds piquancy to the potential monotony of congress not only by varying the permutations of carnal geometry, but by making his sexual world alive, sometimes uncannily so: those glass dildoes take on an animistic life of their own, and everything – a turtle dove, a candle, a fruit, a yardarm, the tail of a purring cat, a fledgling sparrow, a mouse in a mill all covered with flour, a monkey, a paint pot – can act as a metaphor for the sex organs, so that everything around the startled Nanna turns wonderfully, or alarmingly, fleshly, becoming a potential pretext for, or adjunct to, sexuality. Aretino's text is saturated not just with the bracingly visual (and of course voyeuristic) aspects of eros but with all the smells and tastes and textures and colours of sex (and food and drink, of course, as one would expect from a man whose letters are full of the tang of lemon or the sweetness of almonds, and include recipes for salad and fulsome thanks for presents of olives, or an enormous cheese). Especially colours: again, his letters dwell on the flesh tints of Titian's paintings and the strange colouristic effects of sunset over the Grand Canal (here again, it is as if Aretino were trying to outdo Titian's skills as a painter in his own word-pictures), and erotic writing must always compete with the image, which, though more directly titillating, is always condemned to be *literal*, in contrast to literature's euphemistic or euphuistic indirections, evasions and seductions. Antonia tells Nanna off for her preciousness, only to succumb to its charms herself: there's no point in trying to call a spade a spade when, in the context of eroticism, everything is not only what it is, but some other thing too.

So Aretino's text is not just pornography but meta-pornography, not just an *ars amatoria* but a set of concise reflections on how to write or speak about sex. And what is refreshingly different about it is the way it avoids the sense of fascinated, hallucinatory isolation (a kind of solipsism, even if it is a solipsism *à deux*, or *à trois*, or even *à soixante-neuf*) that suffuses so much pornographic writing. The 'secret life' of nuns is strangely public, the cloister remarkably open to the world outside (contrast the much fiercer sense of seclusion that weighs on Sade's world, for instance – all those Piranese-like dungeons in isolated châteaux, locked away from the world in forest wastes…). This is not only because the present-day Nanna can aerate, so to speak, the stories she tells with the breeze of a Roman evening, as she sits under her fig tree, or even because some of those tales take place outside the convent. Rather, it is again an effect of the metaphorical nature of Aretino's writing, his eye for a striking simile. Sex here is not just people getting tangled up together; the whole world is drawn into the act, thanks to Aretino's ability to look outwards for the deft, telling comparison. This can be comic, and it can be disturbing. When the nuns and friars, just getting down to business, think they are about to be discovered, they scarper, like frogs all jumping into a pond at the same time. A nicely realistic detail – just as sharply observed, in fact, as a similarly realistic passage in Dante's *Inferno*, where the souls of those damned for bribery and corruption dive into one of the rivers of hell to avoid being tormented by their guardian demons (Canto XXII). This is not to say that there is anything particularly infernal in Aretino's realism, sexual or otherwise: one smell quite absent from *The Secret Life of Nuns* is any whiff of sulphur. But there is a fascinating interweaving of the erotic and the religious, if only because religion was just such an all-pervasive fact of life in sixteenth-century Rome. It is not surprising that the children of nuns and priests are described as the offspring of the *Dixit* and the *Verbumcaro* – i.e., the offspring of the 'he (or she) said' and the word made flesh – as if (this is uneasy territory) pornography were perversely, or subversively, paying homage to an ever-paradoxical theology of radical incarnation. The negative side of such a claim would lie in the way that, in Nanna's discussion, on this first day of the three-day *Ragionamento* ('Conversation', the title under which the text was first published), of what to do with her daughter Pippa, the latter's options seem alarmingly polarised. In George Sand's *Lélia*, the relatively emancipated and sexual woman Pulchérie tells her frigid sister Lélia to 'become a nun', and when this prospect is rejected, she concludes, well, in that case, 'become a courtesan'. But in fact the nun/whore polarisation does not even represent a choice between opposites for Aretino's women, since convent and brothel are more or less identical. (Which raises the problem of where a girl *can* go to escape the phallus, or even the *pastinaca muranese*.)

So one of the pleasures of the conversation between Aretino's wise and amiable whores is the way their talk is dotted with vignettes of contemporary Roman life (the crowds on the Sant'Angelo Bridge, or busy shopping in the Piazza Navona), enriched with Latin tags and scraps of liturgy, a pleasure as much auditory as voyeuristic. Above all, *The Secret Life of Nuns* is alive with the sound of music, from the quick blast on the organ at Nanna's consecration as a nun (a *church* organ, that is, though other, more bodily organs make equally sweet music, especially when nuns and friars all go 'Oh!' together – choral sex, as it were) to the sudden, strangely haunting detail of the choirboys sounding their rattles after services towards the end of Holy Week, when all the bells are silent. (Perhaps, if the wind is in the right direction, Antonia and Nanna can even hear the bare-footed friars singing vespers in the Temple of Jupiter.) These cultural allusions add yet another dimension to Aretino's succinct but appetising way with language, his skill with rhythms, alliteration and assonance, the music of vowels as well as bowels (all those farts...). A translation (yet another *pastinaca muranese*) can only gesture towards this. But even the original seems at times to be pointing to a sensuous realm of music and meaning that goes beyond the merely diagrammatic aspects of its protagonists' sexual antics (inventive though they are even when judged by the more bracing standards of the twenty-first century). Aretino's creatures are delightfully and poly-morphously perverse, just as he himself was called by his contemporaries a *poligrafo*, a writer in many genres (but also, as Federigo Gonzaga admiringly put it, a crowd in himself). The appealing notion of the polyphonic text, which eschews single-mindedness for layered effects of phonetic richness and semantic ambiguity, is still fashionable, and justifiably so. But if there *is* a polyphony in *The Secret Life of Nuns*, it is not in the sex alone, whose variations risk becoming monotonous, but in the wider eros of its language, its music. As Antonia and Nanna sit chatting under their fig tree, a choirboy is being taught his music at the nearby church of Santa Maria Maggiore; he will become, in time, *maestro di capella* at St John Lateran, and will no doubt watch, as did Aretino's two whores, the candles being thrown down from the loggia on Candlemas Day. His name is Perluigi da Palestrina, one of the greatest of Roman polyphonists. In 1584 (Aretino will have been dust for almost thirty years; Antonia and Nanna will no doubt be continuing their fig-tree conversations in another place) he will publish his Latin setting of the *Song of Songs*, more melting in its abandonment than *Tristan*, with a text full of tropes not all that far from some of Aretino's more sensual conceits – but this time, as the directors of skin-flicks say when urging on their jaded actors, *with feeling*. '*Quam pulchra es et quam decora, carissima, in deliciis! Statura tua adsimilata est palmae et ubera tua botris. Dixi: Ascendam in palmam et apprehendam fructus eius; et erunt ubera tua sicut botri vineae, et odor oris tui sicut odor malorum. Guttur tuum sicut vinum optimum*': 'How fair you are, how beautiful! O Love, with all its rapture! Your stately form is like the palm, Your breasts are like clusters. I say: Let me climb the palm, Let me take hold of its branches; Let your breasts be like clusters of grapes, Your breath like the fragrance of apples, And your mouth like choicest wine.' Now *that's* a polyphony worth drinking to: *that's* erotic.

– Andrew Brown, 2004

Note on the Text:
I have used the text in Aretino, *Ragionamento. Dialogo*, ed. by Nino Borsellino (Milan: Garzanti, 1984). The translation of the text from the 'Song of Songs' (Vulgate: *Canticum Canticorum*, 7: 4–9) is that of the *Tanakh* (Philadelphia and Jerusalem: The Jewish Publication Society, 1985).

This translation has benefited immeasurably from the expert eye and astute suggestions of Alessandro Gallenzi: my thanks to him.

The Secret Life of Nuns

Pietro Aretino to his darling little monkey[1]

Hail, monkey! Hail, I say – since Fortune holds sway also in the realm of beasts, and thus has brought you from your place of birth and handed you over to me, who realised that you were a great lord in the shape of an animal, just as Pythagoras was a philosopher in the shape of a cockerel, and therefore have dedicated to you the labours, or rather the pastimes, of eighteen mornings – not as if I were dedicating them to an ape, a monkey, or a baboon, but to a great lord. The reason is this: if I had not learnt from Nature's close companion that you were a great lord, I would have dedicated *The Dialogue of Nanna and Antonia* to a beast. After all, even the Romans, who inflicted the death penalty on the man who killed the crow whose only virtue lay in the fact that it had greeted Caesar, not only had the dead bird carried on a litter by two Ethiopians, with fifes leading the way, but they named the place where it was buried 'Ridicule'. So, given the foolishness of so many ancient sages, that of a stupid modern writer is quite excusable.

But to prove my point that you are indeed a great lord, we will begin by telling you that you have the same shape as a man, and that you are who you are, while they are accounted great lords, and are who *they* are; you, in your gluttony, gobble everything down, and they in theirs devour their food so greedily that gluttony is no longer listed in the seven deadly sins; you steal even such a small thing as a needle, and they shed blood to steal, viewing the place where they commit their crimes in just the same way that you do; they are open-handed, as their subjects will proclaim to anyone who asks, and you are courteous, as anyone can attest who risks trying to seize anything from your claws; you are so lustful that you

3

will commit a lewd act even with yourself, and they, without the slightest sense of shame, resort to their own flesh; your presumption outstrips that of the most brazen-faced, and theirs outstrips that of the most famished; you are always choked with filth, and they are always plastered with ointments; you are always twisting and turning, never at rest, and their brains are as motionless as a turning lathe; your jests keep the populace entertained, and their crazy frolics make the whole world laugh; you are a bore, and they are a nuisance; you are afraid of everyone, and fill everyone with fear, while they scare everyone and are scared of everyone; your vices are beyond compare, and theirs incredible; you pull a face at anyone who does not bring you food, and they do not look favourably on anyone unless he is bringing them something they like; they do not care in the least about the insults poured on them, nor do you about the nasty tricks people play on you. So I will not forget the fact that, just as great lords are rather like monkeys, monkeys, likewise, are rather like great lords. And note, O ye satraps, that among the great lords who resemble Bagattino (for that is the name of my pet), the King of France is not to be included; after all, he makes us divine by adopting the same name that we have, and makes the gods human by refusing to let himself be called a god. But to return to you, Bagattino, I declare that if you were not quite without taste as great lords are, I would try to make some excuse for the licentious language in the work that I am publishing under your auspices (an excuse that will be as much use to this work as is the protection of great lords to the works that every day are unworthily dedicated to them), by referring to Virgil's *Priapea*, and those lascivious things that were written by Ovid, Juvenal and Martial.[2] But since you are as learned as the great lords, I will say no more, expecting as my only reward for

4

making you immortal a bite, which you will give me wherever you fancy; even great lords pay in such coin the authors of the praises that are heaped on them, for no other reason than that they understand their art just as you do. I would have said that their souls are made in the semblance of yours, if it had been a decent thing to say; what I *will* say, however, is that the great lords hide their shortcomings in the books they have written for them, just as you hide your ugliness in the outfit I had made for you.

And now, Most High Bagattino (for this is the way to address great lords who are worthy of such honours as you), take these pages I have written and tear them up; even great lords not only tear up the gifts that they are presented with, but polish their backsides with them, as I was almost about to tell you – to the praise and glory of the stupid Muses who, since with their skirts lifted up they run after great lords, are appreciated by those lords just as you appreciate the Muses. Perhaps – when you read what Nanna has to say about the nuns – you would have people believe that I am as malicious as you are. Nanna is a chatterbox, and she says the first thing that comes to her lips, but the nuns deserve every bit of it, since they make a public exhibition of themselves to the crowd, worse than any hussy from the streets, and since the stench of their corruption has filled the world with Antichrists, they do not allow anyone to breathe the flowers of virginity and appreciate the true brides and handmaidens of God that walk among us. While I think of it, I am filled with contentment by the thought of something holy and sacred that passes through the soul as soon as we reach the places where they live, just as the sweet odour of roses fills the nostrils as soon as we come among them; and who would care to listen to angels, once he has heard these girls singing the holy offices with which they curb God's anger, and persuade him to pardon our faults?

Nanna, indeed, does not speak of the women who observe their oath of chastity, as she herself will say as she tells Antonia her story, but she does talk about those women whose stench is perfume for the Devil. And certainly, how could I dare to adore, or to obey, or to praise, any man other than the Most Christian King Francis, or to sing of any man other than the great Antonio de Leyva, or to praise any duke other than the Duke of Florence, or to extol any cardinal other than the Cardinal de' Medici, or to serve any marquis other than the Marquis del Vasto, or to pay homage to any prince other than the Prince of Salerno, or to make mention of any count other than the Count Massimiano Stampa?[3] So I would never have dared to think, let alone write, what I have set down about the nuns, if I did not believe that the flame of my fiery pen would purge away the stains of shame which their licentiousness has left on their lives. The people who live in convents should be as pure as lilies in the gardens, but they have so besmeared themselves with the world's mire that the very abyss is revolted by them, let alone Heaven. So I hope that my book will be that steel, cruel to be kind, plied by the good doctor when he cuts off the infected limb so that the others will remain healthy.

ANTONIA: What's up, Nanna? Do you think the woebegone expression on your face suits a woman who governs the world?

NANNA: The world, eh?

ANTONIA: Yes, the world. Leave the worrying to me. Only the French pox is on speaking terms with me – apart from that, I can't even get a dog to bark at me. And I'm poor and proud, and if I were to call myself pretty depraved too, I wouldn't be sinning against the Holy Spirit.

NANNA: My dear Antonia, everyone has some problem or other, and there are problems even where you think there is happiness – so many problems that you'd be amazed. Take my word for it: this world is a filthy dump.

ANTONIA: You're right there – at least, it's a filthy dump for me, but not for you: *you* get to enjoy the hen's own milk, and all round the squares and the taverns and, well, just about everywhere, it's nothing but 'Nanna' this and 'Nanna' that; and your house is always as full as an egg, and all Rome makes a right song and dance about you, the way the Hungarians do at Jubilee time[4].

NANNA: That's true. But I'm still not happy, and I feel just like a bride who's sat down in front of a great feast and, although she's starving hungry, is held back by a certain modesty: even though she's occupying the head of the table, she doesn't dare eat. And one thing's for sure, sister: my heart isn't where it might be. And that's that.

ANTONIA: Was that a sigh?

NANNA: Never mind.

ANTONIA: Now you really don't have any reason to sigh. Just you watch out, or God Almighty might give you something to sigh about.

NANNA: But why shouldn't I sigh? My daughter Pippa's aged

sixteen, and here I am, trying to settle her future for her, and one person says, 'Make her a nun: that way you'll save three-quarters of the dowry, *and* you'll add a saint to the calendar!'; another one says, 'Marry her off – after all, you're so rich that you'll never even notice she's cost you a thing!'; and another starts egging me on to make her a courtesan straight away, saying, 'The world's rotten – and even if it wasn't so bad, by making her a courtesan you are in fact making a lady out of her. With what you've already got, and what she'll bring in, she'll be a queen in no time at all.' So I'm at my wits' end. And now you can see why Nanna has her problems, too.

ANTONIA: Problems? For a woman like you, these problems should be relished more than the itchy pimples on a man who comes home to a nice warm fire in the evening, drops his trousers, and starts to give himself a good old scratch. When the price of grain goes up – now *that's* a problem! A shortage of wine is a real headache; having to pay the rent is torture; and what really does you in is when you take a dose of pockwood two or three times a year and *still* can't get rid of the blisters and boils and bloody aches and pains.[5] So I'm frankly amazed that you're bothering your head over such a tiny little thing.

NANNA: Amazed? I don't see what's so amazing about it.

ANTONIA: Look, you were born and brought up in Rome, right? So you ought to be able to rid yourself of those worries about Pippa with your eyes closed. Tell me, weren't you a nun once upon a time?

NANNA: Yes.

ANTONIA: Didn't you have a husband?

NANNA: I did.

ANTONIA: Weren't you a courtesan?

NANNA: I was. Still am, too.

ANTONIA: So, don't you even have the wit to decide which of these three ways of life is the best?

NANNA: *Mamma mia!* No, I don't, actually.

ANTONIA: No? Why ever not?

NANNA: Because the nuns, married women and whores of today have a completely different lifestyle from what they used to have.

ANTONIA: Ha! Ha! Ha! Life's always been the same: people have always eaten, always drunk, always slept, always stayed awake, always gone away, always stood still – and women have always pissed through their crack. And I'd just love you to tell me something about the lifestyle of the nuns, married women and courtesans of your day; and I swear to you, by the seven churches I've vowed to visit this coming Lent, that just a word of advice from me will help you settle the problem of what to do with your Pippa. Now you tell me – since being such a clever clogs has made you what you are – you tell me first of all why you can't make up your mind to send her to a nunnery.

NANNA: That's fine by me.

ANTONIA: Well, go on then, tell me! After all, today's the feast day of Mary Magdalen, our patron saint, so we can take the day off, and even if it *was* a working day, I've got enough bread and wine and cured meat to last three days.

NANNA: You have?

ANTONIA: I have.

NANNA: In that case, today I'll tell you about the nuns' lives, and then tomorrow about married women, and the day after about prostitutes. Come and sit down next to me; make yourself nice and comfy.

ANTONIA: Ooh, that's better. OK, fire away!

NANNA: I have a sudden strong desire to curse the soul of Mr I-won't-say-who, who got me up the duff with that pest of a daughter.

ANTONIA: Don't get all worked up about it.

NANNA: My dear Antonia, nuns, married women and whores are like a crossroads: the minute you come up to one, you spend ages wondering which way to turn; and it often happens that the devil drags you off down the worst one of all, just as he dragged the soul of my sainted father down that particular road the day he made me a nun, plain contrary to the wishes of my mother, may she rest in peace – you must have known her, maybe? Now *there* was a lady for you!

ANTONIA: I did know her, but it was all a bit hazy. And I know, by hearsay, that she used to perform miracles behind the Banchi[6]; and I've also heard that your father, who was a copper[7], married her out of love.

NANNA: Don't remind me, it breaks my heart when I think of it. Rome just wasn't the same place when it was deprived of a couple like those two. Anyway, to get back to what I was saying, on the first of May, Ms Marietta (that was my mother's name, though they teasingly nicknamed her Lovely Tina) and Mr Barbieraccio (that was my father's name) brought together all their family, the uncles and aunts and grandparents and male and female cousins and nephews and brothers, with a host of friends, both men and women, and took me to the nunnery church, dressed all in silk, with amber rosaries round my waist and a golden coif, on top of which was the crown of virginity woven out of roses and violets all in bloom; and I had perfumed gloves and velvet slippers; and if I remember rightly, it was Pagnina, who's just entered the Order of the Penitent, who'd given me the pearls I was wearing round my neck and the gown on my back[8].

ANTONIA: Yes, they can't have come from anyone else.

NANNA: And in all this finery, just like a new bride, I went into the church, where there were thousands and thousands of people; they all turned round to look at me the minute I appeared, and some said, 'What a beautiful bride Sir Lord God is going to get!'; and others, 'What a shame, making such a lovely girl become a nun;' and some of them blessed me, and some devoured me with their eyes, and some said, 'She'll make some friar or other a happy bunny.' But I didn't take these comments amiss, and I heard one person heaving passionate sighs, and I could easily recognise them as coming from the heart of a lover of mine who just couldn't stop crying while they were performing the service.

ANTONIA: You mean you had lovers before you became a nun?

NANNA: Of course! I wasn't a fool, you know. But there was no lust. Anyway, then they placed me in the front row, ahead of the other women; and after I'd sat there for a while, they started to celebrate the mass, and I was made to kneel between my mother Tina and my aunt Ciampolina; and an altar boy sang a little *laude* while he played the organ; and after the mass, once they'd blessed my nun's habit that was lying on the altar, the priest who'd read the epistle and the other one who'd read the gospel raised me to my feet and then made me kneel down again, this time on the steps of the high altar; then the one who'd said the mass sprinkled holy water over me, and sang a *Te Deum* with the other priests with maybe a hundred different kinds of psalms, and they took off my ordinary clothes and dressed me in my nun's habit; and all the people, jostling up against one another, made a noise like the one you hear in St Peter's or St John's when some woman gets herself walled up, either out of madness, despair or cunning – as I once did.[9]

ANTONIA: Oh yes, I can just imagine you, in the centre of all that crowd.

NANNA: After the ceremony, once they'd wafted incense at me, and sung the *Benedicimus* and the *Oremus* and the *Alleluia* over me, a door opened, making the same creaking, groaning noise as the lid of the poor box; then I was lifted to my feet and led to the exit, where some twenty nuns, as well as the Abbess, were waiting for me; as soon as I saw the Abbess, I dropped her a nice curtsey, and she kissed me on my forehead, and said a few words that I didn't catch to my mother and father and other relatives, who were all weeping and wailing, each one louder than the other; and then the door was suddenly slammed shut, and I heard a 'Oh, no!' which made everyone start.

ANTONIA: And where did the 'Oh, no!' come from?

NANNA: From my poor old lover boy. The very next day he had himself made a discalced friar or hermit in sackcloth, if I'm not mistaken.

ANTONIA: Poor bloke.

NANNA: Anyway, when they shut the door – so quickly I didn't even have a chance to say goodbye to my family – I well and truly thought I was going to be buried alive, and I imagined I'd be seeing women as good as dead as a result of all their austerities and fasting; and I stopped crying for my parents and started crying for myself. So I walked along, my eyes fixed to the ground and my thoughts turning to whatever it was that lay in store for me, and came to the refectory, where a whole troop of nuns came running up to hug me, and they immediately started calling me 'sister', which cheered me up a little bit; and once I'd seen a few fresh, glowing, ruddy-cheeked faces, I felt a thousand times better, and looking at them with a little more assurance, I said to myself, 'One thing's for sure: the devils can't be as ugly as they're painted.' Just then, who should come in but a whole crowd of friars and priests, and the odd lay brother too – the most handsome lads you've ever seen, all bright-eyed and bushy-tailed, and each of them took his girlfriend by the hand. They looked like angels leading the celestial dance.

ANTONIA: Hey, just you keep Heaven out of this!

NANNA: All right, they looked like lovers laughing and joking with their nymphs.

ANTONIA: That's a more suitable analogy. Go on.

NANNA: They took their ladies by the hand, and gave them the biggest, sweetest smackers imaginable, competing to see who could give the most honeyed kisses.

ANTONIA: And which men gave the sugariest ones, in your view?

NANNA: No doubt about it – the friars.

ANTONIA: And why's that, do you think?

NANNA: It's all explained in the legend of the Wandering Whore of Venice[10].

ANTONIA: What happened then?

NANNA: Then everyone sat down to one of most exquisite feasts I thought I'd ever seen; in the place of greatest honour sat her ladyship the Abbess, with his lordship the Abbot on the left; and after the Abbess was Sister Treasurer, and next to her the Graduate; opposite sat Sister Sacrestan, and next to her the Novice Master; and there followed, in succession, a nun, a friar and a lay brother, and down at the far end of the table I don't know how many altar boys and other little friars; and I was placed between the preacher and the confessor of the nunnery. And then the food was brought in; believe you me, the Pope himself never ate a meal like it. The minute we fell to, all the chattering stopped – it was as if the word 'Silence', written in the places where the reverend fathers have their rations doled out to them, had imposed itself on every mouth – on every tongue, rather, since their mouths made the same chomping noise as do those of full-grown silkworms when, after a long period of fasting, they gobble up the fronds of those trees under the shade of which that poor chap Pyramus and that poor lass Thisbe used to play around – may God be with them in the next world as he was in this![11]

ANTONIA: You mean the fronds of the white mulberry tree.

NANNA: Ha! Ha! Ha!

ANTONIA: What're you laughing for?

NANNA: I'm laughing at a pig of a friar, God forgive me; even while his jaws were grinding away like two grindstones, and his cheeks were all puffed out like those of a man blowing a trumpet, he still raised a bottle to his lips and swigged the whole lot down.

ANTONIA: *Domine* choke him!

NANNA: Anyway, as soon as they started to feel they'd had enough, they began to natter and chatter, and for me, in the middle of the meal, it was just like being in the middle of the market in Piazza Navona, when on every side you can hear people buying stuff from one Jew or another. And when they were full, they started choosing the tips of chicken wings and a comb or two and maybe a head, and the men would offer them to the women and the women to the men, so that they looked like swallows popping food into the mouths of their baby swallows. And I can't begin to

14

describe the laughter and uproar when they presented each other with a capon's arse. And as for the quarrels they got into as a result... I couldn't describe them.

ANTONIA: How totally gross.

NANNA: I almost threw up when I saw a nun chewing a great mouthful and then feeding it into her boyfriend's mouth with her own mouth.

ANTONIA: Dirty trollop!

NANNA: Well, once the pleasure of eating had turned into that jaded sense that people feel after they've done you know what, they began mimicking the Germans with their toasts; the General picked up a big glass full of Corsican wine, and invited the Abbess to do the same, whereupon he swallowed it down as easily as a false oath. And all eyes were already gleaming from drinking too much, like the glass on a mirror, and clouding over with the fumes of wine, just as a diamond mists over when you breathe on it. Their eyes would have all closed, and the whole assembly, falling into a slumber over their food, would have turned the table into a bed, if it hadn't been for a handsome boy who suddenly came in, carrying a basket covered with one of the whitest and finest linen cloths I thought I'd ever seen. Snow? Hoarfrost? Milk? No, it was even whiter than the full moon, I can assure you!

ANTONIA: What did he do with the basket? And what was in it?

NANNA: Hey, slow down a bit! The boy bowed in the Spanish way they go in for in Naples, and said, 'Good health to your worships!' Then he added, 'A servant of this fine society has sent you fruits from the earthly paradise,' and he uncovered the gift and placed it on the table. And just imagine: there was a roar of laughter as loud as a peal of thunder – in fact, the whole company burst out laughing in just the same way some poor family bursts out crying when they see that their father's eyes have just closed for ever.

ANTONIA: There's something so nice and natural about the comparisons you come up with!

NANNA: Hardly had they set eyes on those fruits of paradise than the hands of the men and the women (already starting to explore each other's thighs and tits and cheeks and piccolos and pussies with the same dexterity as thieves explore the pockets of the stupid wankers whose wallets they snaffle) shot out towards those fruits just as people rush to pick up the candles that are thrown down from the Loggia[12] on Candlemas Day.

ANTONIA: What were these fruits, exactly? Tell me!

NANNA: They were those glass fruits made in Murano, near Venice, shaped like a man's testimonials, except they have two dangling bells that would have done a tambourine proud.

ANTONIA: Ha! Ha! Ha! I catch your drift! I know what you mean...

NANNA: And that woman was in raptures, not to say lucky, who managed to grab the thickest and longest one; and all of them without exception gave theirs a kiss, saying, 'These things diminish the temptations of the flesh.'

ANTONIA: Devil take them, the whole brood of them!

NANNA: I was playing Little Miss Butter-wouldn't-melt-in-her-mouth, while casting the occasional glance at those fruits – in fact, I was just like a wily she-cat keeping one eye on the servant girl and trying with her paw to snatch the piece of meat that the silly lass has gone and left unguarded. And if it hadn't been for the nun sitting next to me, who'd taken two and gave me one of them, I'd have picked up one for myself to show I wasn't completely dumb. To cut a long story short, laughing and chattering, the Abbess stood up, and everyone followed suit; and the *benedicite* she said at table was in the vernacular.

ANTONIA: Never mind the *benedicite*. Once you'd all got up from table, where did you go?

NANNA: That's what I'm coming to. We went into a room on the ground floor, spacious and airy, with paintings on every wall.

ANTONIA: What were the paintings of? The penances for Lent, or what?

NANNA: Penances? Hardly! The paintings were of a kind that would have made even a hypocrite stand and stare. The room had four walls; on the first was the life of St Nafissa[13], and you could see her as a good little girl aged twelve, filled with charity, handing out her dowry to bent coppers and cheaters at dice, parish priests and grooms, and every kind of decent upstanding person; and once she'd dispensed her riches, all humble and compassionate there she sat down, a fine example to us all, in the middle of the Ponte Sisto[14], without the least pomp or circumstance, apart from her stool, her shawl, her little dog and a sheet of paper with curvy edges stuck in the end of a split stick, with which she seemed to be fanning herself and keeping the flies away.

ANTONIA: Why was she sitting there on the stool?

NANNA: She was sitting there to fulfil the charitable task of dressing the naked; there she was, a young slip of a girl like I told you, sitting and looking up with her mouth wide open, just as if she was singing the song that goes:

What is my love doing, and why won't he come?

She was also depicted standing up and turning to a man

who was too bashful to ask her to do him a little favour – and so, filled with feelings of joy and humanity, she went up to him, and taking him to the dark little cell where she habitually comforted the afflicted, first she took the jacket off his back, and then untied his trousers and laid bare his little turtle dove, which she fondled so affectionately that it reared up proudly and, as wild as a stallion that's broken its halter and leaps onto a mare, it thrust its way between her legs. But, reckoning that she was unworthy to look him in the face and perhaps (as the preacher said when he regaled us with her life story) not up to the challenge of seeing it so red and steaming and filled with fury, she turned her back on him in magnificent style.

ANTONIA: May her soul be given this offering!

NANNA: This offering *is* always being given to her soul, isn't it? She *is* a saint, after all!

ANTONIA: True.

NANNA: Who could describe the whole thing to you? One of the paintings showed the people of Israel whom she graciously sheltered and always comforted *amore dei*[15]. And there was a painting of more than one man who, having tasted what was on offer, came away from her holding a fistful of coins which the kindness of others had forced her to take. Indeed, she treated those who had ploughed her as if they were guests in the house of some generous man who not only welcomes them, feeds them and clothes them, but also gives them the wherewithal to finish their journey.

ANTONIA: O pure and blessed lady, St Nafissa, inspire me to follow in your most holy footsteps!

NANNA: In conclusion, everything she ever did, through the front door and the back, inside and out, is here painted quite realistically, and even her last end is depicted, and at her burial are shown all the Eyetie clients she left in this world so as to find them again in the next;[16] and there aren't as many different greens in a May salad as there are varieties of screw, or screwing, in her coffin.

ANTONIA: I really want to see those paintings one day, by hook or by crook.

NANNA: In the second one, there's the story of the mute Masetto da Lamporecchio[17]. I swear to you on my soul that the two nuns look as alive as if they were real – the ones who took him into that hut while the cheeky rascal, feigning sleep, made his shirt stick out like a sail as he hoisted his murderous great yardarm.

ANTONIA: Ha! Ha! Ha!

NANNA: Anyone seeing the other two nuns – the ones who, realising what frisky frolics their fellow nuns were engaged in, decided not to tell the Abbess but to league up with them – just couldn't help bursting out laughing. And everyone was amazed at the sight of Masetto who seemed to be indicating by sign language that he was averse to joining in. Eventually we all stopped in front of the picture of the wise Mother Superior finally deciding to do the decent thing and inviting the valiant man to have dinner and sleep with her. One night, to avoid getting skinned alive, he started speaking, which made the whole neighbourhood come running to witness the miracle. And as a result the nunnery was canonised as a holy place.

ANTONIA: Ha! Ha! Ha!

NANNA: In the third picture were (if I remember correctly) portraits of all the nuns who were ever members of this Order, with their lovers next to them and the children born from their union, with the names of each boy and girl.

ANTONIA: What a fine memorial.

NANNA: In the last picture were depicted all the ways and means in which you can fuck and be fucked; and the nuns are obliged, before they embark on their jousts with their men friends, to try and assume the postures shown as in a *tableau vivant*; this is so that they won't be left looking clumsy in bed, as some women do who just lie there stiff on their backs, not offering the least odour or savour, so that anyone who samples them finds them about as tasty as a bean minestrone without any olive oil or salt.

ANTONIA: So they need a fencing mistress?

NANNA: And a fencing mistress they have, and if they are ignorant, she shows them what to do if lust so inflames a man that he wants to mount them on a chest, on the stairs, on a chair, on a table, or just on the bare floor. And she needs the same patience as anyone training a dog, a parrot, a starling or a magpie when she teaches the good nuns what positions to take up. And it's easier to juggle with little balls than it is to stroke the birdy so that, even if it's not in the mood, it'll stand up straight.

ANTONIA: Are you sure?

NANNA: Sure I'm sure. Anyway, we finally got bored of the paintings and of chattering and joking, and just as the street is soon swallowed up by the Barbary steeds that run in the Palio[18], or, more precisely, just as the cow flesh is swallowed up by those forced to eat in the servants' refectory, or lasagne is swallowed up by a famished peasant – well, just in the same way did the nuns, the friars, the priests and the lay brothers all disappear, not even leaving the altar boys nor the little friars, nor even the man who had brought the glass thingummies. Only the Graduate stayed with me, and as I was all alone, I didn't say a word, but stood there almost trembling. Then he said to me, 'Sister Cristina' (this was the name I had been rebaptised with when I took the veil), 'it turns out that it's my job to take you to your cell, where the soul is saved by the triumphs of the flesh.' But I wanted to keep him at arm's length, and so I adopted a modest expression and kept silent. He took me by the hand, the one holding the big fat glass sausage – which nearly slipped and fell to the ground. I couldn't stop myself grinning wickedly at this, and the holy father thereupon plucked up the courage to kiss me; and since I was born of a merciful mother, not made of stone, I stood still and gave him a sly look.

ANTONIA: A good move.

NANNA: And so I let myself be guided by him, the same way a blind man is led by his bitch. Guess what happened next. Well, he led me to a little room in the middle of all the other ones, and separated from them by a plain brick partition; and the cracks in the wall were so badly plastered that even if you just put the corner of your eye to one of the chinks, you could see everything going on in every nun's little cell. Once I'd gone in, the Graduate was just about to open his mouth to tell me (I imagine) that my charms surpassed those of the fairies, and to utter the words 'my love', 'my sweetheart', 'my dearest', 'light of my life', and so on and so forth, all the usual fiddle-faddle, while arranging me on the bed exactly the way he wanted, when all of a sudden there comes a *knock knock knock* that terrified the Graduate, and everyone else in the convent who heard it, just as a door suddenly flung open terrifies a swarm of mice gathered round a heap of nuts, so that they're paralysed by fear, and can't even remember where they left their mouse holes. It was exactly the same in the convent: everyone wanted to hide and they bumped into each other, all bothered and bewildered as they tried to take cover from the Saffragun[19].

That's who it was – the Saffragun of the bishop in whose protection the convent was; he'd terrified us with his *knock knock knock* the same way as frogs squatting on a tussock, poking their ears up above the grass, are terrified by the sound of a voice or a stone being flung, which makes them dive into the river pretty much almost simultaneously. And as he walked through the convent he was on the brink of entering the room of the Abbess who, in company with the General, was reforming vespers to suit the breviary of her nuns; and Sister Cellarer says that he'd just raised his hand to knock on the door and so on, when he was distracted by someone kneeling at his feet – a nun as learned as Ancroia and Buovo's Drusiana in the art of singing and dancing.[20]

ANTONIA: What a grand scene there'd have been if he'd actually gone in! Ha! Ha! Ha!

NANNA: But good luck was on our side all that day. I say that because the minute the Suffragan had sat himself down…

ANTONIA: Now *that's* how you say it.

NANNA: …well, along comes a Canon, the Deacanon actually,[21] to bring him the news that the Bishop was turning up. So he jumped up and rushed over to the Bishop's Palace to smarten himself up to go and meet him, having first ordered us to celebrate his arrival by ringing the bells. So, as soon as he'd stepped outside, everyone gradually went back to their game; only the Graduate was obliged to go, in the name of the Abbess, to kiss the hands of His Most Reverend Lordship. And when they all appeared before their girlfriends again, they looked like starlings returning to the olive tree that they'd only just been chased away from by the cries of 'Oy! Oy!' from the peasant, who feels it's his own heart that's being pecked whenever a bird pecks one of his olives.

ANTONIA: I'm still waiting for you to get to the nitty-gritty –
like a baby waiting for the wet nurse to shove her titty in its
mouth. And the wait is harder for me, famished for the facts
as I am, than Holy Saturday is to someone peeling eggs after
fasting all through Lent.

NANNA: Let's get to the nub, then. I'd been left all alone, and
I'd already pledged my love to the Graduate, as I didn't
think it right to want to fly in the face of the convent's
customs, and I reflected on the things I'd seen and heard
over the five or six hours I'd been there; and holding in
my hand that glass pestle, I started to gaze at it the way
that someone who's never seen it before stares at that
terrible lizard on view in the Chiesa del Popolo.[22] And I was
perplexed at the sight, which gave me more cause for
wonderment than the bones of the beastly great fish that
was left high and dry at Corneto[23]; and I couldn't for the life
of me work out why the nuns held it so dear. And while
I was trying to get my head round this problem, I heard a
peal of laughter breaking out, so wild it would have cheered
up a dead man. And as the noise kept getting louder,
I decided to see where the laughter was coming from. I got
up, and put my ear to one of the cracks; and as you can see
better in the dark with one eye than with two, I shut my left
eye, and fixed my right eye to the space between one brick
and the next, and what did I see?... Ha! Ha! Ha!

ANTONIA: What *did* you see? Please tell me!

NANNA: I saw a cell with four nuns in it, plus the General and
three novice friars all milky and ruddy-red in complexion,
who were stripping the Reverend Father of his tunic and
dressing him in a satin doublet, covering his tonsure with a
golden cap over which they placed a velvet biretta covered
all over with crystal pendants, and adorned with a white

feather. The General, in raptures, buckled a sword at his side, and started to address everyone in a northern accent, swaggering up and down as if he'd been Bollocky Bartolomeo[24]. Meanwhile the nuns had taken off their habits and the novices their tunics, and the nuns put on the novices' tunics, or rather three of them did, and the friars put on the nuns' habits; the other nun, having swathed herself in the General's cassock, sat in pontifical solemnity and pretended to be the Father laying down the law to the convent.

ANTONIA: What larks, eh!

NANNA: You haven't heard anything yet.

ANTONIA: How's that?

NANNA: The Reverend Father called over the three novice friars and, leaning on the shoulder of one of them, a tall chap for his age, lanky but lithe, got the others to take out of its nest the fledgling sparrow that was all snug and comfy there; then the most knowing and most attractive friar took it in the palm of his hand, and stroked its back the same way you stroke the tail of a cat that purrs and then starts to pant and soon can't keep still – the little sparrow lifted its crest and the valiant General seized the most beautiful and youngest of the nuns, hoisted her tunic over her head, and made her lean her forehead against the bedstead, and with his fingers he gently opened the leaves of her Arsoniensis mass book and, ravished at the sight, contemplated her fanny, which looked neither so scrawny as to be cleaving to the bone, nor so plump as to stick out all over the place, but was somewhere in the middle, quivering and curvy and glistening like a piece of ivory imbued with life. And those little dimples you can see in the chins and cheeks of beautiful ladies were also visible in her lovely little bum cheeks (as the Florentines call them), softer than a mouse in a mill, born and bred in flour; and all the nun's limbs were so smooth that if you'd placed your hand on her loins it would have slipped down to her legs all in one go, faster than your foot slips on ice; and hair would no more have dared grow on her than on an egg.

ANTONIA: So the Father General consumed his day in contemplation, eh?

NANNA: No – not in contemplation, exactly. What he did was pop his paintbrush in her little paint pot, after first moistening it with his spit. Then he proceeded to wiggle it the same way that women do when they are giving birth or suffering from an attack of hysteria. And to make sure that the nail was more firmly driven into the hole, he motioned behind him to his novice bum chum, who pulled his trousers right down to his heels and placed his cryster in his Reverend Lordship's *visibilium*.[25] His Lordship meanwhile fixed his gaze on the other two sturdy young rascals who had arranged two of the nuns all neatly and comfortably on the bed and were pounding their sauce in the mortar – which was enough to drive their sister to despair: being a bit cross-eyed and dark-complexioned, she'd been rejected by everyone, and so she'd filled up the glass John Thomas with the hot water used to wash the hands of His Lordship, plopped herself down on a pillow on the floor, pushed the soles of her feet against the wall of the cell, and lowered herself straight down onto that huge crozier, thrusting it into her body the same way you thrust a sword into a scabbard. I could smell their pleasure; it made me feel more worn down than a pledge from a pawn shop, as I rubbed my monkey with my hand, the way cats in January rub their arses against the rooftops.

ANTONIA: Ha! Ha! Ha! How did the game all end?

NANNA: It was bump and grind for half an hour, and then the General said, 'All together now! And you, my silly little prick, give me a kiss; you too, my dove.' And placing one hand on the angelic little girl's jellybox, and with the other fondling the ruddy apples of the cherub behind him, kissing him and her in turn, he pulled the same grim face as that marble figure in the Belvedere makes at the serpents who are throttling him between his two sons.[26] Finally, the nuns on the bed, and the young lads, and the General, and the girl he was on top of, and the boy behind him, and the lass with the parsnip from Murano, all agreed to sing in unison like singers in a choir, or rather blacksmiths hammering away simultaneously. And so, each of them intent on their task, they came out with cries of, 'ooh! aah!', 'hug me tight!', 'turn round', 'stick your lovely tongue in!', 'give it to me!', 'take it out!', 'push hard!', 'wait a minute, I'm coming!', 'ow, do it to me!', 'hold me!', and 'help!'. The one was murmuring, the other yowling loudly, and they all sounded as if they were singing 'Do-re-mi-fa'; and their eyes were popping out of their heads, and they were panting and writhing and humping and bumping so much they made the benches and chests and bedsteads and chairs and soup bowls shake like houses in an earthquake.

ANTONIA: Blimey!

NANNA: Then eight sighs were breathed all at once, from the livers, lungs, hearts and souls of the Reverend, etcetera – the nuns and the novices, who stirred up such a gust of air they would have blown out eight torches; and as they sighed, they collapsed from exhaustion, like people sozzled by too much wine. As for me, I'd been almost numbed by the discomfort and frustration of watching them do it, and I discreetly withdrew; and I sat down, and started to gaze at that glass thingummy.

ANTONIA: Hang on a bit – how come there were *eight* sighs?

NANNA: Don't be such a stickler for detail! Just listen.

ANTONIA: So tell me.

NANNA: As I gazed at the glass thingummy, I felt a hot flush all over – after all, what I'd just seen would have shaken the convent of Camaldoli[27] itself – and as I gazed, I fell into temptation…

ANTONIA: And *libra nos a malo*[28].

NANNA: … and unable any longer to resist the urgings of the flesh that were goading my nature on like a beast, as I didn't have any hot water like the nun who'd told me what to do with the crystal fruits, necessity was the mother of invention and I pissed into the handle of that spade.

ANTONIA: How?

NANNA: Through a little hole made in it so that it could be filled with warm water. Anyway, why drag the story out? I cheerfully hoicked up my habit, and placed the pummel of the short sword on the box, and placed the point just inside me, and slowly and gently started to massage my monkey. It was itching like billy-o, and the head of the mullet was nice and thick, which filled me with a mixture of pleasure and pain; still, it was more pleasure than pain, and bit by bit the genie entered the bottle. I broke out into a real sweat, and sat astraddle like a knight errant, and stuck it so far up me I almost lost it inside; and as it entered me, I thought I was dying a death sweeter than the life of bliss. And I held the beak of the thing down there in my melting softness, feeling all in a lather; then I pulled it out, and as I pulled it out, I still felt that stinging sensation that a man with the pox has when he stops scratching his thighs. So I take a quick look at it and – it's all bloody! And that made me want to scream out, 'Go on, confess!'

ANTONIA: Why, Nanna?

NANNA: Why, you ask? Well, I thought I'd given myself a deadly wound: I put my hand to my little mouth and dabbled about in the wetness and brought it up to my eyes; and when I saw it all drenched in red like the glove of a bishop in all his finery, I burst into tears. And with my hands tearing at the sparse short hair that was all I'd been left with by the man who vested me in church, I struck up the lamentation of Rhodes[29].

ANTONIA: You mean of *Rome* – that's where we are.

NANNA: OK, have it your way: Rome. As well as being afraid of dying when I saw the blood, I was also frightened of the Abbess.

ANTONIA: What for?

NANNA: What for? Well, once she'd seen what had caused the blood and heard the facts of the matter, she might well have clapped me in jail, bound in chains as a brazen hussy. And even if the only penance she'd given me was to confess to the other nuns why it was I was bleeding, don't you think that would have been cause enough for me to start howling?

ANTONIA: No. Why should it be?

NANNA: What do you mean, 'no'?

ANTONIA: I mean you could have laid the blame on the nun you saw having her bit of fun with the glass thing, and you'd have got off scot-free.

NANNA: Yes – if the other nun had got all bloody like me. No, there were no two ways about it: Nanna really was up shit creek. Anyway, there I was when I heard someone knocking on the door of my cell, so I carefully dried my eyes, got up and replied *gratia plena*; and then I straight away opened the door and realised I was being called to dinner. But since I'd been stuffing myself all morning, not like a novice nun but like a soldier on the pillage, and as my worry about the blood had quite made me lose my appetite, I said I'd rather go without food this evening; and I bolted the door shut, and stood there mulling it all over, with my hand on my fanny. And realising that it had stopped bleeding, I cheered up just a bit; and not having anything better to do, I went back to the chink in the wall that, as I could see, was gleaming with the light of the lamp the nuns lit at nightfall. And as I peeped through it once more, I saw that everyone was naked; in fact, if the General and the nuns and the novice friars had been old folks, I'd have said they looked just like Adam and Eve with the other poor souls in limbo. But let's leave comparisons to the smart alecs. The General then made his bum-chum, that tall lanky chap, climb onto a little square table where the Four Little Christian Sisters of the Antichrist were eating, and instead of a trumpet, he was holding out a rod the same way that trumpeters hold out their instruments, and he proclaimed the tourney; and after the 'tara-ra!' he said, 'The Grand Sultan of Babylon makes it known to all valiant jousters that this very minute they should appear in the lists with their lances couched; and to him who breaks the most lances will be awarded a round and hairless ring, which he will be able to enjoy all night. *Amen!*'

ANTONIA: What a fine proclamation! His master must have given him some notes beforehand. Go on then, Nanna.

NANNA: So all the jousters were lined up ready, and the quintain they'd chosen was the rear end of that cross-eyed, dark-complexioned nun who'd been gorging greedily on the glass thingummy. Then they drew lots, and the first tilt went to the trumpeter. He told his colleague to carry on sounding his trumpet while he went into action, and, spurring himself on with his fingers, he ran his lance right into his lady-friend's target right up to its hilt; and as his thrust was three times as strong as most, he was showered with praise.

ANTONIA: Ha! Ha! Ha!

NANNA: After him, the next lot was drawn by the General; running up with his lance couched, he filled the ring of the man who'd just filled the nun's, and there they stood, fixed as firmly as the boundary markers between two fields. The third tilt fell to a nun, and since she didn't have a fir-tree lance, she took one made of glass, and at the first clash of arms rammed it up the General's backside, squashing its glass ballocks right into her beaver with the best will in the world.

ANTONIA: Just the thing!

NANNA: Then along came novice number two, since the lot had now fallen on him, and his very first shot scored a bull's-eye; and the other nun, mimicking her colleague with the lance and its two balls, plunged it straight into the young man's *utriusque*, making him wriggle like an eel when he received the impact. Then came the last man and the last woman, and we had good reason to laugh uproariously, since she buried the pastry she'd feasted on that morning into her lady-friends's ring; and he, standing behind the rest of them, planted his little lance in her backside, so that they all looked like a row of kebabbed souls that Satan was roasting on the fire for Lucifer's infernal carnival.

ANTONIA: Ha! Ha! Ha! What a feast!

NANNA: That cross-eyed nun was the life and soul of the

party, and while everyone was playing rumpy-pumpy, she kept coming out with the funniest jokes you've ever heard; and when I heard them, I laughed so much that they heard me, and realising that I'd been heard, I withdrew. And I don't know who it was started to shout, and after a short while, when I went back to my little spyhole, I found it covered by a sheet, so I couldn't see how the joust ended, nor who won the prize.

ANTONIA: You've let me down just at the best bit.

NANNA: I've let you down because *they* let *me* down. I was pissed off at not being able to see the spurt of the bean seed and the chestnut seed. Anyway, as I was saying, there I was, feeling really cross with myself for laughing and so depriving myself of a seat at the sermon, when what did I hear…

ANTONIA: What *did* you hear? Go on, tell me!

NANNA: I could see three cells through the chinks in the walls of mine…

ANTONIA: Those walls really were full of holes – holier than a sieve!

NANNA: In my view, they didn't exactly take much trouble to fill them in, and I guess the nuns enjoyed watching each other. Be that as it may, I heard a panting, a sighing, a grunting and a pawing that seemed to be coming from ten people or so all suffering from some nightmare. I stood listening (it was right opposite the partition dividing me from the scene of the jousts) and heard a low murmuring; so I placed my eye to the chinks in the wall, and what do I spy but two little nuns, all fresh and curvaceous, with their legs in the air, displaying four fat round thighs that looked like clotted cream as they wobbled so furiously; and each of the nuns was holding her glass carrot. Then the one said, 'They must be really crazy, thinking that our appetites can be satisfied by these crappy little things – they can't kiss, and don't have any tongues, or any hands to play our keyboards with, and even if they did, if we feel so turned on by artificial thingies, what would we do with real live ones? We can well call ourselves poor fools if we end up wasting our youth on bits of glass.' 'You know, sister,' replied the other, 'if you want my advice, you'll come with me.' 'And where are you off to?' said she. 'As soon as dusk falls, I'm going to scarper from this convent and head off with a young man to Naples; he's got a friend, a blood brother, who'd be just the thing for you. Come on, let's get out of this hole, this tomb, and make the most of our youth the way all women should.' And her friend didn't need much persuading, since she was easily led, and she accepted the invitation – they sealed the agreement by hurling the glass lances against the wall, covering the noise of the shattering glass by shouting, 'Cats! Cats!', pretending that some cats had broken their water jugs and everything else too. Jumping out of bed, they first bundled up their best clothes, and then slipped out of the cell together, and I was left behind. Then all of a sudden there came the sound of palms striking on one another, a cry of 'Oh, I'm just *so* unhappy!', a face being scratched, and a tearing of hair and garments, all most strange; and I swear on my honour that I thought the bell tower had caught fire. So I peeped through the gap between the chinks, and saw that it was Her Ladyship the Abbess who was uttering the Lamentations of Jeremiah the Apostle.

ANTONIA: What do you mean, the Abbess?

NANNA: The devout mother of the nuns and the protectress of the convent.

ANTONIA: What was wrong with her?

NANNA: All I could think of was that her confessor must have murdered her.

ANTONIA: How?

NANNA: Their little game had just been coming up to the grand finale when he took his stopper out of her bunghole and tried to shove it into her stinky winky. The poor woman, all a-lather and as horny as hell, love juice pouring out of her, fell on her knees at his feet and begged him by the Stigmata, the Sorrows, the Seven Joyful Mysteries, the *Pater Noster* of St Julian[30], the Penitential Psalms, the Three Wise Men, the Star and the *sancta sanctorum*, but she just couldn't get that Nero, that Cain, that Judas to shove his leek back into her little garden; no, with a face as grim as Marforio[31], filled with venomous rage, he forced her with menacing words and gestures to turn right over; he made her stick her head in a small stove and, hissing and spitting like a deaf asp, and foaming at the mouth like a great orc, he planted his sapling shoot in her restorative compost heap.

ANTONIA: Filthy bugger!

NANNA: And he really started to enjoy himself pushing it in and pulling it out – he would have gone to the gallows a thousand times for it; he was laughing at the noise he could hear as his pole went in and out, like the *slip*, *slop* and *slap* that pilgrims' feet make when they trudge down a road so clogged with mud and clay that it often pulls their shoes off.

ANTONIA: He deserves to be hanged, drawn and quartered!

NANNA: The poor woman was inconsolable: with her head in the stove, she looked like the soul of a sodomite in the Devil's mouth. Finally the Father, deigning to hear her prayers, told her to take her head out, and without pulling his key out of the lock, that frigging friar carried her on his rod over to a trestle; he draped the poor martyr over it and started to wriggle about more vigorously and deftly than a man playing the keys of a clavicembalo[32]; and as if her joints had come apart, she turned right round and tried to drink in her confessor's lips and eat his tongue, meanwhile sticking out hers – it looked exactly like a cow's; and she gripped his hand with the flaps of her valise, and made him twist and turn as if she'd grabbed him with a pair of pincers.

ANTONIA: I'm gobsmacked – this is like dying and going to heaven!

NANNA: So, withholding as long as he could the floodwaters that set the mill wheel in motion, that holy man finally brought his labours to completion; he wiped his rope with a perfumed handkerchief, and the good woman cleaned out her honeypot, and they took a breather and then gave each other another hug, and the greedy friar asked her, 'Did it seem right and proper, my little pheasant, my pea-hen, my dove, my soul of souls, my heart of hearts, light of my life, that your Narcissus, your Ganymede[33], your angel should not be able for once to resort to your hindquarters?' She replied, 'Did it seem right and proper, my gosling, my swan, my falcon, my consolation of consolations, my delight of delights, my hope of hopes, that your nymph, your handmaid, your bit of fun should not be able just on one occasion to place your natural in her nature?' And she lunged forward at him and bit him, leaving the black marks of her teeth on his lips, so that he let out a dreadful shriek.

ANTONIA: What a hoot!

NANNA: After that, the prudent Abbess grabbed his relic, and stretched out her mouth to it and gave it a long slow kiss; then, quite enamoured of it, she started munching it and nibbling it the way a puppy dog will nibble your legs or your hands, so that you enjoy his bites – they make you laugh and cry at the same time. In the same way, that randy friar was in raptures at our lady's pecks and bites and kept saying, 'Ooh! Aah!'

ANTONIA: Stupid minx. She could have torn a piece off with her teeth.

NANNA: While the good Abbess was playing so kindly with her adored idol, there came a soft knock at the door of her cell. They both froze. As they stood there stock-still, listening, they heard a really faint whistle, and then they realised it was the confessor's novice, so they opened up and he came right in; and since he knew the cut of their jib, they weren't in the least dismayed. Indeed, the treacherous Abbess, dropping the Father's chaffinch and picking up the lad's goldfinch by its wings, longing to rub the bird's bow over her lyre, said, 'My love, do me a favour, will you darling?' The naughty monk said to her, 'Gladly. What can I do for you?' 'I want,' said she, 'to grate this cheese with my cheese grater; at the same time, I want you to place your harpoon in the drum of your spiritual son; and if you enjoy that enjoyable experience, it'll be gee up, Dobbin! And if not, we'll try every which way – there's bound to be *one* that suits us.' Meanwhile, Brother Galasso had lowered the sails down from the young lad's skiff, and seeing this, madam sat herself down, opened wide her cage, popped the nightingale inside her, and pulled the whole burden on top of her, to the great delight of all present. I can tell you, she was on the verge of busting a gut, with that great mound on her belly, kneading her the way a piece of cloth is kneaded and kneaded at the fuller's. Finally she shot her load, and they fired their crossbows, and now the game was over, they swigged down so much wine and wolfed down so many pastries I lost count.

ANTONIA: And how could you rein in your desire for a man, seeing so many keys going into so many keyholes?

NANNA: My love juices were really pouring out of me at the sight of the abbatial assault, and since I was still holding the glass dagger...

ANTONIA: I can imagine you gave it a good sniff or two as you held it, the way people sniff a carnation.

NANNA: Ha! Ha! Ha! I was well frisky after seeing those battles, so I emptied the cold urine out of the clapper, and filled it up again; then I sat on it. Once I'd stuffed the bean into the bean pod, I could easily have gone to push it right up my arsenal, since I'll try anything once – after all, you never know quite which way's going to be best.

ANTONIA: Good idea. I mean, it *would* have been a good idea.

NANNA: So, rubbing myself up and down on its ridge, I felt my front door starting to tingle very pleasantly, thanks to the burnisher that was burnishing my bucket; and as I was in two minds, pondering whether or not I should take the whole argument on board or just part of it, I think I would have let the dog slip into its kennel if I hadn't happened to hear the confessor, who together with his pupil had got dressed again, asking the Abbess, now fully satisfied, whether he couldn't head off, so I hurried over to see her billing and cooing as he took his leave. She went all babyish and started cajoling him and saying, 'When are you going to come back? Oh my God, aren't you the one I love, aren't you the one I adore?'; and the Reverend Father was swearing by all the saints and by the second coming that he'd be back the very next evening; and the young lad, who was still doing up his trousers, gave her a kiss with his tongue in her mouth, to say goodbye. And I heard the confessor, as he left, starting to intone the *pecora campi* they sing at vespers.

ANTONIA: What? That charlatan was pretending to say compline, was he?[34]

NANNA: Got it in one. And no sooner had he left than I heard such a clatter of feet that I realised the jousters too had finished their day's labour and were on their way home bearing their prizes, making their horses piss beforehand so that it reminded me of the first showers of August.

ANTONIA: Bloody hell!

NANNA: But just you listen to this. The two nuns who had bundled up their things had gone back to their rooms; and the reason, as far as I could tell from their grumblings, was that they had found the back entrance locked on the Abbess' orders, and this made them call down more curses on her than the wicked will endure at the Last Judgement. But their excursion wasn't in vain, since as they went down the stairs they saw the muleteer having a nap, the one who'd entered the service of the convent two days before, and they started to have designs on him. So the one said to the other, 'You can go and wake him up and tell him to bring an armful of firewood to you in the kitchen; that way he'll think you're the cook, and he'll get a move on; then you can show him this cell and tell him, "Put it in there," and once the rascal is inside, just let him give your little sister a good time.' Her advice didn't fall on deaf ears, and was immediately followed. But just then I discovered another complication.

ANTONIA: What did you discover?

NANNA: I discovered, next to the cell those nuns were in, a room decorated like a courtesan's, all in fine boxwood, very neat and pretty, in which there were two holy sisters; and they'd laid a little table, a lovely sight it was, and placed on it a tablecloth that looked like white damask, and it smelled more nicely of lavender than muskrats smell of the musk they make. They'd laid it with napkins, plates, knives and forks for three persons, so clean and dainty that I couldn't describe them, and then they took out of a little basket many varieties of flowers, and went round decorating the table with them, taking the greatest care over it all. One of the sisters had arranged in the middle of the table a showpiece bouquet all in laurel leaves, and strewn it with some white and red roses so that they stood out to greatest effect; and they had decked out the ribbons used to tie up the bouquet with orange blossom – the ribbons extended the full length of the table. And in the bouquet they had written, in borage flowers, the name of the Bishop's vicar, who that very same day had arrived with his Monsignore: and it was more for the vicar than for his mitred lord that the bells were sounding, and their *ding dong* prevented me from hearing a host of interesting things I could have told you about. Anyway, it was for the vicar that the wedding feast was being prepared, as I was saying – this was something I found out later. Now the other nun had decorated every corner of the table with something really beautiful; on the one corner she arranged a Solomon's knot in violet gilly flowers; on the second, a maze of elder-tree flowers; on the third, a heart shape of deep red roses, pierced by a dart made from the stem of a carnation, with the arrow point made by its bud – half open, it looked as if it were drenched in heart's blood. And above this, she had arranged bugloss flowers to represent her eyes red from weeping, and the tears they shed were made of those little orange buds just freshly opening on the tips of their branches. On the last corner she had arranged two hands in jasmine, clasped together, with a *fides* of yellow gilly flowers. After this, one of the nuns started to wash some glasses with fig leaves, and burnished them so well that they seemed to have been transformed from crystal into silver; her colleague, meanwhile, had set on a small shelf a fine Rheims linen cloth, and placed the glasses in order of size on this sideboard; then she set in their midst a pear-shaped carafe filled with orange water, from which was hanging a soft fine-woven towel that she had put there for people to dry their hands; it looked like the bands of the mitre that hang down from a bishop's forehead. At the foot of the sideboard was standing a copper basin; it had been so well polished with sand, vinegar and elbow grease that you could see your own reflection in it. Filled to the brim with fresh water, it contained two little phials of smooth glass that seemed to be holding not red or white wine but distilled rubies and topaz. And when all this had been set out, she took from out of a chest a loaf of bread that looked like a wad of cotton wool, and handed it to another nun, who put it in its correct place. And then they took a short rest.

ANTONIA: You have to admit that only nuns could have taken such pains to make the table look nice: they have nothing better to do with their time.

NANNA: There they were sitting, and the bell chimed three o'clock; then the boldest of them said, 'The vicar is taking longer than the Christmas mass!' 'It's hardly surprising that he's late,' said the other: 'the Bishop is intending to preside over a confirmation tomorrow, and must have given him some errand or other.' Then they started chattering and nattering about one thing after another so that the wait would pass more quickly, and so the time went by; and then they both started to lay into him till they were blue in the face, slagging him off just the same way that Master Pasquino runs down priests:[35] they called him a good-for-nothing, and a pig, and a rascal (a fine birthday present!), and one of them ran over to the fire where there were two capons being boiled, so huge and gouty that they couldn't move; standing guard over them was a spit bent in the middle under the weight of a peacock that they had raised; and she'd have chucked them all out of the window if her colleague hadn't stopped her. And in the middle of this argy-bargy, the muleteer who was supposed to unload the firewood in the cell of the nun who had been given such good advice by her soul sister – well, he went to the wrong door, despite the fact that she'd shown him which one to go to when she'd loaded the wood on his back. And going into the room where His Lordship was expected, the silly ass dropped off his load of firewood right there. When they heard him doing this, the two nuns went berserk, scratching their faces and tearing at their whole bodies.

ANTONIA: What did they have to say about the young dibbler?

NANNA: What would you have said?

ANTONIA: I'd have seized the opportunity.

NANNA: That's just what they did. Delighted at the unexpected but timely arrival of the muleteer, just as pigeons are delighted to find some food, they gave him a right royal welcome, and barring the door so the fox wouldn't escape from the trap, they made him sit down at table between them, rubbing him all over with a towel fresh from the laundry. The muleteer was twenty or so years old, clean-shaven, florid and plump, with a forehead like the base of a bushel, with two great thighs like an abbot's – a sturdy chap, white-complexioned, the sort that shoots first and asks questions afterwards, a real party animal: too good for them. He roared with laughter like a great baboon when he saw himself being set down in front of all the capon and peacock, and he started gobbling it down in great mouthfuls, and swigged at the wine like a peasant at harvest time. The two nuns meanwhile, starting to think they'd have to wait a thousand years for him to curry-comb their coats with his clapper, turned their noses up at the food as if they weren't hungry; and if the greediest of them hadn't lost patience like a starving hermit, and swooped down on his fife like a vulture on a chick, the muleteer would have just gone on stuffing his face like a coach driver. No sooner had he been touched than he popped out a lance piece that would have outdone that of Bevilacqua[36]: it looked like that trumpet that the man at the Castle waves about before blowing it;[37] and while the one nun held his great rod in her hand, the other pushed the table away. Then her accomplice took the little chap between her legs and lowered her whole body down onto the muleteer's flute as he sat there; and when she started pushing with all the discretion of the crowd of people that push each other over Sant'Angelo Bridge after the benediction, they all fell down, the chair, the muleteer and she, too: they fell backwards like a crowd of monkeys, and once the key had slipped out of its lock, the other nun, who was slobbering at the chops like an old mule, afraid that the little chap might catch cold now that he wasn't wearing anything on his head, covered him with her graceful whatyamacallit. Meanwhile her comrade, finding herself deprived of the bung in her hole, flew into a rage, grabbed her colleague by her throat, and made her puke up the little that she'd eaten; the latter then turned on her, without even bothering to reach her journey's end, and they thrashed each other more than if they'd been Holy Pauls[38].

ANTONIA: Ha! Ha! Ha!

NANNA: Well, the big booby was just getting to his feet to break up the brawl when I suddenly felt someone placing his hands on my shoulders and saying in an undertone, 'Good evening, sweetheart!' I jumped and shook all over with fear – all the more scared since I'd been so intent on the deeds of arms being performed by those horny bitches (if you'll pardon the expression) that I'd stopped thinking about anything else at all. So when I felt someone touching my back, I turned round and said, 'Who the hell?…' and just as I was opening my mouth to shout, 'Help!' who did I see but the Graduate who had left me to go to meet the Bishop, so I calmed down. Then I said to him, 'Father, I'm not one of those women, as you seem to think – just you keep your distance! I don't want to, so watch it, or I'll scream; I'd rather let you slit my wrists – God protect me! I'll never do it, never! No I won't, do you hear? You ought to be ashamed of yourself. Wonderful – I'm going to tell everyone!' Then he replied, 'How can it be that in a cherub, in a throne, in a seraph there should reside such cruelty? I am your servant, I adore you: you alone are my altar, my vespers, my compline and my mass, and whenever it please you that I should die, here is my knife; plunge it into my breast, and you will see in my heart your sweet name written in letters of gold.' With these words he tried to press into my hand a beautiful knife with a handle of gilt silver, its blade finely decorated for half its length in damascene work; I refused to take it from him, and without a word continued to gaze at the ground; then, uttering those exclamations that are sung at the *passio*, he kept on at me so much that I finally gave in.

ANTONIA: Those who allow themselves to be persuaded to kill and poison men do much worse; and you did a more

charitable deed than any pawnshop; and all women of
worth should follow your example. Go on!

NANNA: Well, having let myself be won over by his friar's
preamble, in which he trotted out more lies than a clock that
doesn't tell the right time, he flipped me over and climbed
on top of me with a *laudamus te* as fervent as if he were
blessing the palms on Palm Sunday, and with his songs and
chants he so enchanted me that I let him have his way...
But what do you think I should have done, Antonia?

ANTONIA: Exactly what you did do, Nanna.

NANNA: I mean he came in through the front door. And
would you believe it?

ANTONIA: What?

NANNA: The thing made of flesh seemed to me less painful
than the thing made of glass!

ANTONIA: Never! Who'd have guessed it!

NANNA: No, I swear by this cross here, it really was!

ANTONIA: No need to swear – I totally believe you, I really do.

NANNA: I pissed without pissing...

ANTONIA: Ha! Ha! Ha!

NANNA: ...this kind of white sticky stuff, like a snail's slime.
Anyway he did it to me three times, if you'll forgive me
saying so: twice in the old way and once modern style; and
as for this last custom, whoever invented it, well, I don't like
it, I swear I don't, not one little bit.

ANTONIA: You're wrong.

NANNA: We're up shit creek if I'm wrong. Whoever invented
it can't have had much of an appetite – and not much taste
either, unless it was for... But don't make me say it.

ANTONIA: Don't badmouth it. It's a titbit that attracts more
customers than lamprey. It's a dish for connoisseurs.

NANNA: They're welcome to it. Anyway, as I was saying:

when the Graduate had planted his standard twice in my fortress and once in my ravelin, he asked me if I'd had dinner yet, and since I could tell from his breath that he'd stuffed himself as full as a Jew's goose, I told him that I had. Then he pulled me back onto his lap, and put one arm round my neck, and with his other hand he fondled first my cheeks and then my titties, punctuating his caresses with the most savoury kisses imaginable, so that I started giving thanks in my thoughts for the hour and the minute I'd been made a nun; I'd come to the conclusion that the true paradise was the one the nuns lived in. As we sat there, the Graduate suddenly had a bright idea, and he wondered whether to take me on a tour round the whole convent. 'We can sleep it off all day tomorrow,' he said; and now that I had witnessed so many miracles in four different rooms I was impatient to witness countless more in the others. He shook off his shoes and I slipped out of my slippers; he held my hand and I followed him, stepping along as gingerly as if I had been walking on eggs.

ANTONIA: Go back a bit.

NANNA: Why?

ANTONIA: Because you've forgotten those two nuns left high and dry by the muleteer's mistake.

NANNA: Oh dear, I really must have left my brains at home. Those poor, unfortunate creatures quenched their fury on the knobs of the firedogs. They pushed them inside themselves and started hopping and jumping around on them like condemned men impaled by the Turks; and if the one of them who finished her little jig first hadn't come to the aid of her little friend, the knob would have come right up through her mouth.

ANTONIA: Oh what a big one it must have been! Ha! Ha! Ha!

NANNA: I slipped after lover boy as smoothly and quietly as oil; and then we came to the cell of the cook, which the absent-minded ninny had left half open, so we peeped in and saw her having a good time, going at it doggy-fashion like a bitch in heat with a pilgrim who had (I imagine) been asking her for alms so he could visit St James's in Galicia, whereupon she'd invited him in. And his long pilgrim's cloak was lying on the back of the chest, folded up, and his staff, from which was hanging a tablet with miracles on it, was leaning against the wall, and a she-cat was toying with his wallet, filled with crusts of bread – the jovial lovers, busied as they were, didn't pay any attention to it, nor to the little cask that had tipped over and was spilling wine everywhere. We were in no mind to waste our time watching such lumpish lovemaking, but then we came to the chinks in the wall of Sister Cellarer who, having lost all hope of her parish priest arriving, had been driven so mad that she'd tied a rope to a beam, climbed onto a trestle and looped the rope round her neck. She was just about to kick away the support from under her, and was already opening her mouth to say 'I forgive you' to the priest when he, arriving at the door and pushing his way in, came inside and saw her about to end it all – whereupon he flung himself on her and threw his arms round her, and said, 'What's all this, then? So, my darling, you think I'm a betrayer to my sworn oath? And where is your God-given prudence? What have you done with it?' At these sweet words, she lifted her head, like those who have fallen into a dead faint do when you splash cold water into their faces, and the sensation returned to her body as it does to a person's frozen limbs when they are placed in front of a blazing fire; and the priest threw the rope and the trestle to one side, and sat her down on the bed; and she gave him a kiss and slowly said to him, 'My prayers have been answered, and I want you to make a wax statuette of me and place it before the image of St Gimignano[39], with an inscription reading "She commended herself, and she was delivered;"' and with these words, she hung the merciful priest on the crosspiece of her gallows. He, soon sated with the first mouthful of she-goat, asked for kid instead.

ANTONIA: I meant to tell you, and then I forgot: call a spade a spade, and say 'arse,' 'prick', 'cunt' and 'fuck', otherwise the only people who'll understand you will be the scholars of the Capranica think tank[40] – you and your 'rope in the ring', your 'obelisk in the arsenal', your 'leek in the garden', your 'bolt in the door', your 'key in the lock', your 'pestle in the mortar', your 'nightingale in the nest', your 'sapling in the ditch', your 'syringe in the flap-valve', and your 'sword in the sheath'; and the same goes for 'the stake', 'the crozier', 'the parsnip', 'the little monkey', 'his thingummy', 'her thingummy', 'the apples', 'the leaves of the mass book', 'that thingy', 'the graceful whatyamacallit', 'that whatsit', 'that doings', 'that latest news', 'the handle', 'the dart', 'the carrot', 'the root' and all the other shit that comes out of your mouth, but there you go, pussyfooting around. Let your yes mean yes, and your no, no, and otherwise, just shut it.

NANNA: Don't you know that it's nice to talk proper in a whorehouse?

ANTONIA: Say it whatever way you want to, then, and don't get cross.

NANNA: Well, as I was saying, having obtained his dish of kid and stuck the blade into the meat it was meant for, he was enjoying himself like someone crazed as he watched it going in and out; and pushing it in and pulling it out gave him as much intense pleasure as a baker's boy gets out of plunging his fist in and out of the dough. In short, our rector Arlotto[41], testing out the stiffness of his poppy stalk, carried the nun wriggling like an eel on it over to the bed, and stamping his seal in her wax with all his strength, he made her roll from the head to the foot of the bed and then again from the foot to the head; and then they were up, and then they were down, and one minute it was the nun who was squeezing the priest's doings, and the next it was the priest who was squeezing the nun's. In this way, with a 'you do it to me' here and an 'I'll do it to you' there, they rolled around so much that the floodwaters finally burst: they drenched the bedsheets like a river overflowing into the plains, and then let go of each other, falling to either side of the bed, panting like a bellows that the worker has just abandoned so that they wheeze to a halt with a great sigh. We just couldn't stop laughing when the key slipped out of the lock and the venerable priest signalled the event with such a fearsome fart (saving your nose) that it echoed throughout the convent, and if we hadn't stopped each other's mouths with our hands, we'd have been discovered.

ANTONIA: Ha! Ha! Ha! It's enough to make anyone dislocate their jaws with laughing.

NANNA: So we left the little gossip to her own affairs and groped our way along and saw the novice mistress dragging out from under a bed a porter who was filthier than a pile of rags, and she was saying to him, 'Out you come, my Trojan Hector, my noble Orlando[42]; behold, I am your servant, and please forgive me for the discomfort I inflicted on you when I had to hide you – I had no choice.' And the rapscallion, waving his rags and tatters, replied with a gesture from his member, and she didn't have an interpreter to explain his secret message, but translated it as the fancy took her; and the bumpkin, thrusting his pruning-hook into her hedge, made her see stars, thousands of them; and his wolfish fangs fastened on her lips so tenderly that he was already making her weep buckets of tears. Then, not wishing to see the strawberry ending up in the bear's jaws, we went somewhere else.

ANTONIA: Where did you go?

NANNA: To a chink in the wall that one of the nuns showed us – she looked like the stern mother of discipline, the aunt of the Bible and the mother-in-law of the Old Testament, so that I could hardly bear to look at her: on her head she had some twenty hairs, like the bristles on a brush, all full of lice, and perhaps a hundred wrinkles on her forehead; her eyebrows were bushy and white, and her eyes were oozing with some yellow stuff.

ANTONIA: You do have sharp eyes, if you can even make out lice at a distance.

NANNA: Just you listen. She had a slobbering, snotty mouth and nose, and her jaws looked like the comb made of a bone, with just two teeth to it, of the sort used by the lice-ridden; her lips were dried up and her chin was pointed like a Genoese's head – its only adornment was a few hairs sprouting out of it like those of a lioness, but (I can well imagine) as prickly as thorns. Her tits dangled down like the scrotum of a man without balls, and seemed to be attached to her chest by two strings; her belly (*miserere!*) was covered with pustules and all sunken, while her navel stuck out. To tell you the truth, around her piss-hole she had a garland of cabbage leaves that you'd have said had been sitting on the head of some scurvy fellow for a whole month.

ANTONIA: Even St Onuphrius wore a bush round his privies, like the one outside taverns.[43]

NANNA: Good for him. Her thighs were spindles covered with parchment, and her knees trembled so much that she always seemed on the point of toppling over. You can imagine what her shins and her arms and her feet looked like, though I must tell you that her fingernails were as long as the one the Ruffian wore on his little finger, as a weapon, though hers were caked with filth.[44] Anyway, she was bending down over the ground and with a stick of charcoal drawing stars, moons, squares, circles, letters and a load of other cock-and-bull nonsense; and as she did so, she summoned the devils by certain names that the devils themselves would never have managed to remember; then, turning three times round those magical symbols, she looked up to the sky, muttering and mumbling; then she took a figure made out of fresh wax into which a hundred needles had been stuck (and if you've ever seen a mandrake, you'll know what I'm talking about) and set it close to the fire so that it could feel the heat, and turning it over and over the same way that ortolans and warblers are turned so that they can get cooked without being burnt, she uttered these words:

Fire, my fire, oh slay
The cruel man who's gone away;

Turning it round with more fury than people giving out bread at a poorhouse, she added:

May my itch, all tingling,
Bring my god of love a-running!

49

The image was beginning to get really hot, and she said, staring fixedly at the floor:

Demon, make him come, my joy,
Back to me – or let him die!

At the end of these little rhymes, lo and behold, along came someone knocking at her door, panting like a man who, on being discovered wreaking havoc in a kitchen, has taken to his heels to save his back from a drubbing; she immediately put her magical implements and spells away and opened the door to him.

ANTONIA: Even though she was naked?

NANNA: Even though she was naked, and the poor man, in thrall to black magic just as hunger is in thrall to famine, threw his arms round her neck; and giving her a long lingering kiss just as if she had been Rosa and Arcolana, praised her beauty to the skies in the same way that those men do who write sonnets to Lorenzina and her ilk;[45] and the accursed hag, writhing all over with pleasure and delight, said to him, 'Should this flesh of mine have to sleep alone?'

ANTONIA: Yuk!

NANNA: I'll not make your stomach turn any more with this old witch from Trento[46]: I don't know what happened to her, since I didn't want to watch any more. And when the bewitched young lay brother, still sprouting his first beard, started to screw her on a stool, I did what Masino's cat did when she shut her eyes so as not to scare off the mice.[47] Anyway, let me tell you the rest of the story. After that old crow, we came to the seamstress, who was engaged in a tussle with the tailor, her master. She had stripped him bare, and was kissing his mouth, his nipples, his rod and his drum, just like a wet-nurse kisses her nursling child on his little face, his sweet mouth, his dainty hands, his nice little belly, his delightful little dangler and his lovely bum, so passionately that it looks as if she wants to suck him the same way that he sucks her titties. Naturally, we wanted to put our eyes to the chinks in the wall and have a squint at the tailor as he tore the hem off the seamstress' tunic, but we heard a cry, and after the cry a shout, and after the shout an 'oh!', and after the 'oh!' an 'oh God!' that pierced our hearts. So we hurried over to the place where the voices were coming from (they made such a noise that they covered the clatter of our feet), and there we saw a woman who had half a baby emerging from her warehouse; then she pissed it right out, head first, to the accompaniment of a volley of perfumed farts. And as soon as they saw it was a baby boy, they summoned his father, the Reverend Guardian, who came along accompanied by two middle-aged nuns. And on his arrival, they immediately threw themselves into every kind of lordly amusement. The Guardian was saying, 'Since on this table there are pen, paper and ink, I'm going to draw up his horoscope.' So he drew a million dots and joined them up with different lines, saying heaven knows what about the house of Venus and Mars, and then he turned round to the rest of the gang and said, 'You should know, sisters, that my son according to nature, flesh and spirit will be a Messiah, an Antichrist or Melchizedek[48].' And the Graduate, wanting to see the crack the baby had emerged from, tugged on my habit, but I shook my head to tell him I didn't want to see any more black pudding except that from a gutted pig.

ANTONIA: Well, that's nuns for you!

NANNA: Just you listen to this. Six days before me, a certain girl had been put by her brothers in the convent where I was to be placed – I won't say she was a virgin, but between you and me she was certainly hot stuff; and feeling mistrustful, since one of the local bigwigs had fallen in love with her (so I was told), the Abbess kept her in a room all by herself; and every night she locked the door and took away the key. And the young lover, having noticed that the barred window of her cell looked over the garden, climbed up the wall to this window like a woodpecker and, once in, he pecked away at the goose for all he was worth. This very same night, the one I'm telling you about, he came to her, and he was giving his hound a drink from the cup she held out to him, with his arms wrapped round the treacherous bars. The honey was just pouring into the gooey pastry when this sweet dessert suddenly turned more bitter than any medicine.

ANTONIA: How?

NANNA: The unfortunate chap had such a turn when he shouted, 'Come on! I'm coming!' that his arms lost their grip and he fell from the balcony onto a roof, from the roof onto a henhouse, and from the henhouse to the ground, with the net result that he broke his thigh.

ANTONIA: I only wish that witch of an Abbess had broken both of hers! Fancy wanting a girl to preserve her chastity in a bordello!

NANNA: She behaved that way out of fear of the friars, who had sworn they'd burn her alive, and the whole convent with her, if they heard so much as a whisper of scandal. Anyway, as I was saying, the young man who had been forced to work like a doggy for his pleasures, woke up everyone, and all the nuns came running to the windows, where they lifted the blinds and in the moonlight made out the unhappy man, all battered and bruised. They got two lay brothers to leave the beds where they were lying with their... ahem... *wives*, and sent them out into the garden, where they picked him up in their arms and carried him off. You don't need me to describe the commotion this caused all round the neighbourhood. After this scandal, we went back into our cells, for fear that the dawn might catch us spying on the doings of others; then we heard a friar, a regular party animal, a greasy, sweaty chap, telling a story to I don't know how many nuns and priests and lay brothers who'd been playing dice and cards all night, and when they'd finished swigging down the vino, they'd started to have a good old natter, and had begged the friar to tell them a story. He replied, 'I will tell you a story – one that began in laughter and ended in tears – all about a big bad dog who was also something of a stud.' His listeners fell silent at his request, and he began: 'Two days ago, I was walking across the square and stopped to look at a little bitch in heat who had two dozen pesky pooches gathered around her, attracted by the smell of her vulva, which was all swollen, and so red that it looked like flaming coral. They kept sniffing at her, now one dog and now another, and a big crowd of children had gathered to see it all. First one dog would mount her and thrust in her a couple of times, and then another dog would do the same and give her another couple of pokes. At this diverting sight I pulled the stern face you would expect of a friar, when suddenly along came a huge farmyard mastiff who looked as if he was the boss of all the slaughterhouses in the world. He seized one of the dogs and dragged him down to the ground in a fury; then

53

he turned his attentions to another, and left great gashes in his pelt – whereupon there was a general rout, as the dogs scarpered in every direction. And the mastiff, arching his back, his hair bristling like a boar's, with squinting eyes, grinding his teeth, growling loudly, foaming at the mouth, glared at the unhappy bitch. And after sniffing her lovely little buttonhole for a while, he gave her two thrusts that made her howl like a full-grown bitch, but she managed to slip away from under him, and made a run for it. And the pooches who were all standing round keeping guard trotted after her; the mastiff, enraged, went off in pursuit, and then the bitch, catching sight of a gap in a closed door, darted through it, and the pooches with her. The vile brute of a dog was left outside all alone, since he was such a huge size that he couldn't squeeze in through the hole the others had slipped through; so there he stood, gnawing at the door, pawing at the ground, and roaring like a lion with a fever. After quite a while, one of the poor pooches emerged, and the lousy dog grabbed him and clawed off a whole ear. When the second appeared, he gave him an even more hostile reception, and one by one he lay into them all as they slunk out, and he made them flee the locality, just as peasants all make a run for it the minute soldiers appear on the scene. Finally, his mate herself came forth, and seizing her by the throat, he sunk his fangs into her windpipe and throttled her, which sent the children scuttling away together with the whole crowd of people who'd gathered to witness this canine fiesta; and they screamed to high heaven as they ran...' After this story, not much interested in seeing or hearing anything else, we went to our room and had a mile's worth of rough-and-tumble in bed before going to sleep.

ANTONIA: Mr Hundred Tales will have to forgive me, but he may as well take early retirement.[49]

NANNA: I don't agree. What I *will* say is that he should at least admit that my stories are real live events, and his are just… stories. But wasn't there something else I still had to tell you?

ANTONIA: What's that?

NANNA: I rose at nones, sensing for some reason that the cock of my parish had slipped away early, and I went off to have lunch, where I couldn't stop myself grinning maliciously at the sight of those nuns who had spent the night in the carnal town of Capernaum[50], and in a few days I was on good terms with all of them, and it became clear to me that, just as I'd seen them, they'd all seen me too – when I was fooling around with the Graduate, I mean. When we'd finished lunch, a Lutheran[51] friar climbed up into the pulpit; he had a voice like a nightwatchman, so strident and thunderous that you could have heard it from the Capitoline Hill to Testaccio.[52] And he exhorted the nuns so eloquently that he would have converted the Morning Star.

ANTONIA: What did he have to say?

NANNA: He said that in the eyes of Nature there was nothing more hateful than seeing people wasting their time – the time that she has given us to pass in pleasure and delight. And she rejoices to see her creatures increase and multiply, and above all else she is delighted when she sees a woman who, having reached old age, can say, 'World, you may go in peace.' And Nature holds dearer than all other women the little nuns who feed sugared titbits to the God of Love; so the pleasures she grants to us religious folk are sweeter a thousand times over than those she gives to women of the world. And the friar loudly proclaimed that the children born to a friar and a nun are the offspring of the *Dissit* and the *Verbumcaro*.[53] Then he even went into the delicate loves of flies and ants, and worked himself up into a real passion – as if all the words that came from his lips were being uttered by the mouth of truth. People with nothing better to do listen attentively enough to a street singer, but those good house-wives listened even more attentively to that blatherer. And he gave the blessing with one of those things – you know what I mean: made of glass, three spans long – and came down from his pulpit; and to quench his thirst he swilled down the wine the way horses swill down water, and gobbled up the pastries as greedily as a bollocky donkey gobbles vine leaves. And they gave him more presents than a priest singing mass for the first time receives from his relatives, or a newly-wed daughter from her mother. And then he went away, and each of the nuns occupied herself with some trifling errand or another. I went back to my room, and before long I heard a knock at the door, and who did I see but the Graduate's young servant. With a courteous bow he handed over to me something wrapped up and a letter folded the same way as those feathered arrows with three corners – or grooves, I should say – that you find on the arrowheads. The superscription said… I don't know if I'll remember the exact words… wait a bit, yes, I've got it:

> *May these few plain and simple words of mine,*
> *Written in tears and then dried by my sighs,*
> *Be handed to the Sun in paradise!*

ANTONIA: That was lovely!

NANNA: Inside, there was a long rigmarole that went on and on; it began with my hair, which had been cut off in the church, and said that he had gathered it together and made a neckband of it for himself; and my forehead was clearer than a cloudless sky. He compared my eyebrows to the black wood which is used to make combs, and he said that my cheeks were so white that they filled milk and cream with envy. He declared my teeth were like a row of pearls, and my lips like pomegranate blossoms; he composed a great preamble on my hands – he even praised my finger-nails; and he said that my voice was like the canticle *Gloria in eccelsis*; and when he came to my breasts, he waxed positively ecstatic – they displayed two apples as white and shining as the snow in sunlight. Finally he allowed himself to slip down to the fountain, saying that he had drunk from it all unworthily, and that it distilled nectar and manna, and that the curls of hair round it were made of silk. As for the reverse of the medal, he kept shtum – his excuse was that Burchiello[54] would need to be born again to describe even the minutest particle of it, and he concluded by giving me thanks *per infinita secula*[55] for the liberality with which I had bestowed my treasure on him, and swearing that he would soon come to see me; and with a 'farewell, my lovely,' he signed off with these words:

> *The man who's most alive when on your breasts,*
> *Impelled by love, his love for you attests.*

ANTONIA: And who wouldn't have hoicked up her skirts in response to such a delightful song?

NANNA: When I'd read this latest communication, I folded the paper and, before tucking it away in my bosom, I kissed it; and unwrapping the parcel, I saw that it was a really lovely little prayer book that my dear friend had sent me – at least, I *thought* it was a lovely little prayer book. It was covered in green velvet, which was meant to signify love, and its ribbons were all of silk. I picked it up, smiling, and turned it over, gazing at it delightedly, kissing it repeatedly and praising it as the loveliest I had ever seen. I sent the messenger away, telling him that he should kiss his master on my behalf; then, as soon as I was alone, I opened that little book to read the *Magnificat*, and as soon as I opened it, I saw that it was full of illustrations showing the ways that clever nuns manage to enjoy themselves. I burst out laughing when I saw one of them: with her assets poking out of a basket whose bottom had been knocked out, she was lowering herself from a rope onto the round pointy bit of a whacking great rod. This made me laugh so loud that one of the nuns who was closer pals with me than any of the others came running up. 'What are you laughing at?' she asked me, and I didn't need to have my arm twisted to tell her everything; I showed her the little book, and we had such fun looking through it that it gave us a great desire to try out the positions illustrated, which meant we had to use the glass handle. My little friend placed it so snugly between her thighs that it looked like a man's thingummy pointing straight up at the place of temptation. So I lay down there and then, like one of the ladies from the Santa Maria Bridge[56], and put my legs on her shoulders, and she stuck it in me, first in the right way and then in the not-so-right way, and soon brought me off; and then she lay down the same way that I had, and in return for my tart she gave me a pastry.

ANTONIA: Do you know, Nanna, what occurs to me when I hear you talking?

NANNA: No.

ANTONIA: The same thing that occurs to someone who catches a whiff of a laxative: without actually needing to take it, off he goes to dump his load a good two or three times.

NANNA: Ha! Ha! Ha!

ANTONIA: I have to say that your tales seem so vivid and lifelike to me that you've made me piss myself even without having to taste truffles or cardamom.[57]

NANNA: You told me off for talking indirectly, and then you go straight ahead and use the same language as people putting riddles to little girls and saying, 'I have a thing which is as white as a goose, but it's not a goose, so tell me what it is!'

ANTONIA: I talk this way to please you – that's why I use obscure expressions.

NANNA: Thank you. Anyway, let's finish the anthem! After we'd disported ourselves in this way for a while, we felt like exhibiting ourselves at the grating and the turnbox.[58] But we couldn't get close, since all the nuns had hurried over there just as lizards when they come running out to bask in the sun; and the church was as crowded as St Peter and Paul's on the day they do the Stations of the Cross, and even monks and soldiers were being granted an audience; and take my word for it, I swear I saw the Hebrew Jacob who was chatting to the Abbess quite unconcernedly.

ANTONIA: The world's gone to the dogs.

NANNA: You're telling me. Anyone who wants it can have it. I even saw one of those unhappy Turks who got himself caught in the net, in Hungary.

ANTONIA: They should have made a Christian of him.

NANNA: Well, either way, I saw him, whether he'd been baptised or not I can't say. But I was a proper fool to promise to describe to you in just one day the life led by the nuns: in a single hour, they get up to so many things that it would take a whole year to relate them all. The sun is getting ready to set, so I'll cut things short and make like the horseman who's in a hurry to gallop off – he's starving hungry, but he just grabs four quick bites, swigs a hasty drink, and then he's off.

ANTONIA: Let me tell you one little thing. You said to me at the start that things ain't what they used to be in your day: I was imagining you were going to tell me about the nuns of yore, as their deeds are related in the works of the Holy Fathers.

NANNA: My mistake, if I did say anything of the kind. Maybe what I meant was that the nuns aren't what they used to be in the old days.

ANTONIA: So it was a slip of the tongue, not a deliberate mistake.

NANNA: Either way, I've completely forgotten. Let's get back to the main point – much more important! As I was saying, the devil tempted me, and I let myself be saddled by a friar who'd just arrived from the University, though I had to keep an eye open for the Graduate. And as Fortune would have it, he would often take me out to dinner outside the convent, quite unaware that the Graduate and I were an item. And it turned out that he came to see me one evening after the *Ave Maria*, quite unexpectedly, and said, 'My darling little cherub, be so kind as to do me a favour and come along with me to a place where you'll have a really good time; you'll hear not just angelic music, but also see a really splendid comedy being performed.' I was never one to resist temptation, so without a moment's hesitation I undressed, and he gave me a hand; I took off my nun's habit and put on perfumed clothes – I mean the boy's clothes that my first lover had had made for me; and on my head I placed a little bonnet of green silk, with a red feather and a golden clasp, and with a cloak on my back, I went off with him. We hadn't walked a stone's throw before he turned into a long and very narrow alley, only a couple of feet wide, that led to a dead end; and he gave a long, low whistle, and we heard someone quickly coming down a stairway and opening a door. No sooner had we crossed the threshold than there appeared a pageboy holding a candelabrum with white wax candles. We climbed the stairs by its light, and appeared in a beautifully decorated hall. My student friend was holding me by the hand. The pageboy with the candelabrum lifted the curtain covering the door into the room, and told us, 'Please go in, Your Lordships.' So we went in, and as soon as I was inside, I saw all the people there stand up, cap in hand, as do congregations when the preacher gives his blessing. This was a refuge for all those in holy orders who wanted to screw in peace, a real knocking shop; here came all sorts and conditions of nuns and friars, just as every kind of witch and warlock resorts to the walnut tree at Benevento.[59] And everyone sat down, and all you could hear was people whispering about my sweet little face – for though it shouldn't be for me to say, you ought to know, Antonia, that it *was* beautiful.

ANTONIA: That I can well believe – you're really beautiful even now you're an old woman, and you must have been a really beautiful girl.

NANNA: In the midst of all these compliments, along came the virtue of music that pierced me to the depths of my soul. There were four of them, reading the music from a book, and another one, with a silver lute in tune to their voices, was singing 'Divine and shining eyes…' Then there came a woman from Ferrara who danced so wonderfully that she aroused the admiration and astonishment of all present: she cut capers that a kid goat wouldn't have managed – with such skill, my God, with such grace, Antonia, that you wouldn't have had eyes for anything else. What a marvel it was to see her, tucking in her left leg like a crane, and standing entirely poised on her right leg, then spinning like a top, so that her skirts, ballooning out as she spun round and round, unfurled in a lovely circle; she went so fast that you couldn't see her any more than you can see the weathervanes on some shack when they are blowing in the wind – or rather, it was like the paper windmills made by children and stuck onto the end of a stick: the kids hold them at arm's length and start to run along, since they love to see them whirling round and round, so fast they're almost invisible.

ANTONIA: Ah, God bless her!

NANNA: Ha! Ha! Ha! I'm laughing at another chap, 'Giampolo's son' they called him – he was a Venetian, I imagine – he slipped behind a door, and mimicked a whole host of voices. He could do a porter so well that any fellow from Bergamo would have had to own himself beaten;[60] and the porter, asking an old woman for the lady of the house, took off the old woman saying, 'And what do you want with Her Ladyship?' To which he replied, 'I'd like to speak to her.' And the wicked man then said to her, 'My lady, oh my lady, I'm dying, I can feel my lungs boiling up like a panful of tripe.' He poured out his complaint to the old woman in the funniest way imaginable. And he started touching her up a bit, and laughing and coming out with all sorts of merry sayings tailor-made to make her spoil her Lenten observance or break her fast. And as he blathered on, suddenly her old husband, gone a bit soft in the head, caught sight of the porter and made such a commotion that he resembled a peasant seeing his cherry tree being plundered; and the porter said to him, 'Sir, oh Sir! Ha! Ha! Ha!', laughing and gesticulating and playing the fool, and the old man retorted, 'Off you go, for God's sake, you drunken ass!' And he told his maidservant to pull off his shoes, and told his wife I don't know what, all about the Sultan and the Great Turk; and he made everyone there piss themselves laughing when, taking off some of the straps he used to belt his waist in, he swore that he would never eat windy foods again; and then he let them put him to bed, and fell asleep and started snoring, whereupon the other chap returned disguised as the porter, and with the lady of the house he laughed and cried so much that he was soon stroking her little fur coat.

ANTONIA: Ha! Ha! Ha!

NANNA: Yes, and you really would have laughed if you'd heard the noise they made when they bumped their things together, especially as the porter punctuated the proceedings with his wicked words, which fitted in all too well with those uttered by Lady Do-it-to-me. Once this singing of vespers was over, we returned to the room where there was an alcove for those who were going to perform in the comedy. The curtain was just about to rise when someone started hammering on the door, since given the noise everyone was making with their chattering, he would never have made himself heard if he'd knocked softly; and so they let the curtain fall, and they opened up to the Graduate. For it was he – the same who, happening to pass by, had knocked on the door, quite unaware that I was cheating on him. And coming upstairs and seeing me making out with the student, he was overwhelmed by the blows of that cursed hammer of jealousy that knocks all men blind senseless, and filled with the same fury that drove the mastiff to kill the bitch (as the friar's story related), he seized me by the hair; he dragged me through the hall and down the stairs, ignoring the prayers and supplications that everyone made on my behalf – except, that is, for the student who, the minute he spotted the Graduate, vanished like a spark from a Catherine wheel; and he pulled me along back to the convent, beating me all the way, and in the presence of all the nuns he forced me to climb on someone's back and gave me a flogging, as gently as friars when they punish one of their inferiors for spitting in church. And the blows he administered to me with the straps from the lectern came so fast and furious that the flesh of my buttocks was flayed, a good span of it. But the thing that hurt me the most was that the Abbess sided with the Graduate. Then, after a week spent rubbing ointment into my wounds and bathing myself in rose water, I sent a message to my mother saying that, if she wanted to see me alive, she should come straight away, and finding me barely recognisable, she thought I'd fallen ill as a result of my abstinence and all the early morning masses, and she swore by all the saints that I should be taken home that very minute – and neither the pleas of the nuns nor the monks could succeed in getting me to stay a single day longer. Once I was at home, my father, who was more scared of my mother than I am of anything, immediately wanted to run to get the doctor, but she wouldn't let him, for fear of starting a scandal. And since I couldn't hide the wounds on my backside, where the strap had whirled and twirled like the choirboys' rattles do over the altar steps and at the church doors in the evenings after services in Holy Week,[61] I said that in order to mortify my flesh I'd been sitting on the carding prong they use for oakum – hence my wound. My mother smiled maliciously at this feeble excuse, since real carding prongs would have pierced me through to the heart, not just gone through my arse (may yours be ever safe and sound). But she decided it was best to keep quiet.

ANTONIA: I'm starting to think that you're right when you say you might have a few problems if you make a nun of Pippa; and now I think of it, my mother (may her soul rest in peace) used to say that a nun in a certain convent would pretend every third day that she was suffering from every conceivable illness, just so the doctors would put the urinal up her skirts.

NANNA: I know very well who that was, and it was only for lack of time that I left out her story. Anyway, now that I've kept you entertained here all day long with my chattering, I'd like you to come home with me this evening.

ANTONIA: If you like.

NANNA: And you can help me do a bit of sorting out, and then tomorrow, after breakfast, in this vineyard of mine, beneath this very same fig tree, we'll embark on the life of married women.

ANTONIA: Your wish is my command!

And with these words, not bothering to load themselves down with anything from the vineyard, they went off to Nanna's house, which stood on the Via della Scrofa. They reached it just as night was falling, and Pippa gave Antonia a lovely warm welcome. And when supper time came, they had supper; and then they stayed up chatting for a while. And so to bed.

NOTES

1. Aretino's dedication to his pet monkey (which he calls a Barbary ape and a bogey or monster, among other things) establishes ironic and rather laboured parallels between monkey and man.

2. These Roman writers all satirised (and/or enjoyed depicting) sexual licence: Ovid (46 BC–AD 17) in the *Art of Love*; Juvenal (*c.* AD 55–140) in the *Satires*; Martial (*c.* AD 40–104) in the *Epigrams*. The attribution of the *Priapea* to Virgil (70–19 BC) is apocryphal.

3. Aretino knew many Renaissance statesmen personally. His list here includes: Francis I, King of France; Antonio da Leyva (head of the Imperial army in Italy, Governor of Milan, d. 1536); Alfonso d'Avalos, Marquis del Vasto (another general of the Spanish troops in Italy and another, later, Governor of Milan, d. 1546); Ferrante Sanseverino, Prince of Salerno (whose failure to deliver the pension he had awarded to Aretino led to a break between the two); Count Massimiano Stampa (governor of the castello in Milan, favourite of Duke Francesco Sforza and a friend and protector of Aretino).

4. There is a Jubilee every twenty-five years in Rome, and those who make a pilgrimage to the city in that year, or undergo some similar penance, are awarded a plenary indulgence by the Pope.

5. Pockwood was a decoction of guacum (more precisely, *guaiacolum officinale*, known in Renaissance Italy as *legno santo* or 'holy wood') – a treatment for syphilis.

6. The Via dei Banchi was one of Rome's red-light districts.

7. Nanna's father was a member of the 'bargello' or citizens' police.

8. Pagnina was a well-known courtesan in Rome at the time, and did indeed enter the Ordine delle Convertite.

9. This is a reference to an event in Aretino's third *Dialogue*. St John's is presumably St John Lateran.

10. *La Puttana Errante* ['The Wandering Whore'] was written by Aretino's secretary, Lorenzo Veniero.

11. The tale of Pyramus and Thisbe is told in, for example, Ovid's *Metamorphoses*, IV, lines 55–166. These lovers from Babylon, forbidden to marry by their families, arranged to meet under a white mulberry tree outside the city. Thisbe was attacked by a lion before managing to escape, but Pyramus, seeing her bloodied cloak, thought she was dead and killed himself; finding him dying, Thisbe did the same.

12. Presumably the loggia of St John Lateran or St Peter's.

13. St Nafissa is an imaginary saint, frequently referred to as the patron saint of prostitutes.

14. The Ponte Sisto, a bridge across the Tiber, was near a beggar's hospice in an ill-famed area of Rome.

15. 'with the love of God' (Latin).

16. Aretino here uses the word Eyetie meaning, in fact, French, hinting at all the people St Nafissa has killed by French disease.

17. Masetto da Lamporecchio is the protagonist of a story in Boccaccio's *Decameron* (III.1): he pretends to be a mute and thus, as in Aretino's retelling, gains access to a convent and dallies with the nuns.

18. The Palio is the famous equestrian competition held in Siena.

19. Nanna sometimes uses colloquial (or dialectal) forms of words, or garbles them, as here where she uses *safruganio* for *suffraganeo*, i.e. suffragan, an assistant bishop.

20. Ancroia was the protagonist of a popular verse narrative; the beautiful Drusiana (or Drusania), daughter of the King of Armenia, was the lover and then wife of Buovo (or Bovo) of Antona, in a tale of chivalry; she could sing and play the harp very well.

21. Nanna says first *canonico* then *primocerio* (for *primicerio*); the latter word indicates the man in a religious house who is in charge of wax ('cera'), candles, tapers, etc.

22. Aretino is referring to a marble bas-relief representing a winged dragon in the Roman church of Santa Maria del Popolo.

23. Corneto is modern-day Tarquinia, just up the coast from Rome.

24. The great condottiere Bartolomeo Colleoni (1400–75), immortalised in the equestrian statue by Andrea del Verrocchio in Venice, was associated with balls both because of his name (Colleoni sounds like '*coglioni*', bollocks) and because he apparently shared a peculiarity that ran in the male line of his family: he had three testicles.

25. Nanna says *cristeo* for *clistere*, i.e. clyster, and as elsewhere uses a Latin term as a sexual euphemism (here the word *visibilium*, from the Creed, also has a nicely solemn ring to it, befitting His Lordship).

26. The statue of Laocoon being strangled by sea-serpents between his two sons, placed by Pope Julius II (1443–1513) in the Vatican Museum.

27. Camaldoli is the site near Arezzo in Tuscany where, on a wooded mountainside, St Romuald of Ravenna (d. 1027) founded a monastery that became famed for its austerity. The Order of the Camaldolese still exists.

28. 'deliver us from evil' (Latin). Antonia mispronounces the first word, which should be 'libera'.

29. There was a 'lament of the Grand Master of Rhodes' current in the sixteenth century. Antonia's correction reminds the reader of the many 'laments of Rome' that were composed following the catastrophic sack of the city in 1527, only a few years before the publication of Aretino's *Ragionamento*.

30. Pilgrims seeking hospitality would recite this prayer in honour of St Julian the Hospitaller.

31. Marforio, like the more famous Pasquino, was an ancient statue in Rome used to post satires and denunciations.

32. Another name for the harpsichord.

33. In Greek mythology, both Narcissus and Ganymede were beautiful youths. Narcissus fell in love with his own reflection and pined away; Ganymede was abducted by Zeus and made cupbearer to the gods on Olympus.

34. The words '*pecora campi*' ('the beasts of the field') occur in the Vulgate of Psalm 8, sung at Vespers; compline is the last of the canonical day hours, said before turning in for the night.

35. Pasquino was the Roman statue (disinterred in 1501) used to post satires, especially against members of the Papal Curia and other well-known personalities. Aretino himself contributed to the genre of the pasquinade.

36. Bevilacqua was a noted swordsman.

37. The 'Castle' is Castel Sant'Angelo, the great round fortress on the Tiber, near the bridge of the same name mentioned a couple of lines further down.

38. The Holy Pauls were a fraternity of beggars who were always beating each other up out of envy.

39. St Gimignano was Bishop of Modena (d. 387) and patron of the homonymous town in Tuscany.

40. The Almo Collegio Capranica, or Collegio della Sapienza, was a board of theological and canonical studies founded by Cardinal Domenico Capranica in 1457.

41. This is a reference to Arlotto Mainardi (d. 1484), a churchman famous for his buffoonery.

42. In Greek legend, Hector (husband of Andromache), killed by Achilles, is the bravest Trojan; Orlando is the Italian form of Roland, the hero of numerous medieval romances.

43. St Onuphrius, a hermit, wore vegetation round his loins. The word 'bush' here means (first and foremost) a tavern sign (as in 'good wine needs no bush').

44. The Ruffian is probably a generic rather than a particular term.

45. Rosa and Arcolana were two Roman women of Aretino's day famous for their beauty (again these are possibly generic names). Lorenzina was a real courtesan of Rome.

46. Apollinaire (1880–1918) claims that the area around Trento, and the Tyrol in general, was notorious for its witches and warlocks.

47. This derives from a proverbial expression: Masino's cat shut its eyes and the mice thought it was asleep.

48. Melchizedek was the 'King of Salem' and 'Priest of the Most High God'; his priesthood was seen as prefiguring that of Christ, and a heresy current in the Renaissance actually identified him with Christ or the Holy Spirit.

49. This is a reference to Giovanni Boccaccio (1313–75), author of the *Decameron*, which was also called the *Centonovelle* ('Hundred Tales').

50. Capernaum was the site of Jesus' headquarters and the object of his wrath. On the Day of Judgement, Sodom and Gomorrah will get off more lightly.

51. Aretino's use of the word Lutheran, in this dialogue and other of his works, seems to imply 'shady', 'ideologically unsound'.

52. The Capitoline Hill (Campidoglio) was the centre of ancient Rome; the Testaccio is a hill of broken pottery shards, here representing Rome's periphery.

53. *Dissit* is garbled for Latin 'dixit' ('he said'), *Verbumcaro* is a conflated form of '*et verbum caro factum est*', 'And the Word was made flesh' (John 1:14).

54. Domenico di Giovanni (1404–48), called 'Il Burchiello' ('alla Burchia' = 'any old how') was a writer whose work was so hermetic as to appear as nonsensical.

55. 'for centuries without end' (Latin).

56. The Santa Maria Bridge was another resort of Roman prostitutes.

57. Truffles and cardamom are aphrodisiacs, so Antonia has 'pissed' herself in the frequent sense intended by Aretino, i.e. she has come.

58. Nuns would go to a parlour to talk to their friends and family through a grating and receive gifts through a turnbox.

59. Benevento, in the Neapolitan Appenines, was another resort of witches and warlocks.

60. In the area around Venice and Padua, Bergamo was seen as a good source of porters and other menials.

61. To mark the last days of Lent, the bells in Roman churches were silent from after the *Gloria* of Holy Thursday to the *Gloria* of the Easter Vigil; instead, the end of evening services was marked by the rattling sound of a wooden *crepitaculum*.

BIOGRAPHICAL NOTE

Pietro Aretino was born in Arezzo – from which he took his name – in 1492, the son of a cobbler. Very little is known of Aretino's early childhood, and it is possible that he had no formal education, though by the age of twenty he is known to have been living in Perugia, possibly as a student of art, where his first poems were written.

In 1517, he moved to Rome, where he lived with the wealthy patron Agostino Chigi, and became known at the Court of Pope Leo X. Here Aretino began writing satirical pieces, based on Court gossip and political affairs, and soon came to the notice of the papal aspirant Cardinal Giulio de' Medici. Giulio became his patron for a brief time during the conclave of 1521, in the hope that Aretino might enhance his chances of election by attacking his rival candidates. Both patron and poet were disappointed, however, by the election of the conservative Pope Adrian VI.

After this disappointment, Aretino moved away from Rome to Mantua for a time, and sought new patrons, including the mercenary leader Giovanni de' Medici ('dalle Bande Nere'). He returned to Rome in 1523, when Giulio was elected Pope Clement VII, but was forced to leave briefly the following year after publication of *I sonetti lussuriosi*, a collection of sonnets based on pornographic engravings by Giulio Romano. Aretino's popularity and notoriety grew, and he continued to circulate his satirical poetry and polemic letters – for which Ariosto gave him the title 'Scourge of Princes' – and, in 1525, he completed his popular comedy *La cortigiana* ['The Courtesan']. In 1527, however, he was forced to leave Rome permanently, when an assassin of Bishop Giovanni Giberti, one of his satiric targets, stabbed and almost killed him.

Aretino moved to Venice, where he spent the remainder of his life, and where he produced the majority of his writings, including the *Ragionamento* ['Conversation'] (1534), and *Dialogo* ['Dialogue'] (1536), and the plays *Il marescalco* ['The Farrier'] (1533) and *La Talanta* (1542). He continued to be a prolific letter-writer and was able to live partly on the income provided by the placatory gifts of his correspondents and targets, including, in 1533, King Francis I of France, who presented him with a gold chain. Aretino died in Venice, probably from an apoplectic fit, in 1556.

Andrew Brown studied at the University of Cambridge, where he taught French for many years. He now works as a freelance teacher and translator. He is the author of *Roland Barthes: the Figures of Writing* (OUP, 1993), and his translations include *Memoirs of a Madman* by Gustave Flaubert, *For a Night of Love* by Emile Zola, *The Jinx* by Théophile Gautier, *Mademoiselle de Scudéri* by E.T.A. Hoffmann, *Theseus* by André Gide, *Incest* by Marquis de Sade, *The Ghost-seer* by Friedrich von Schiller, *Colonel Chabert* by Honoré de Balzac, *Memoirs of an Egotist* by Stendhal, *Butterball* by Guy de Maupassant and *With the Flow* by Joris-Karl Huysmans, all published by Hesperus Press.

HESPERUS PRESS CLASSICS

Hesperus Press, as suggested by the Latin motto, is committed to bringing near what is far – far both in space and time. Works written by the greatest authors, and unjustly neglected or simply little known in the English-speaking world, are made accessible through new translations and a completely fresh editorial approach. Through these classic works, the reader is introduced to the greatest writers from all times and all cultures.

For more information on Hesperus Press, please visit our website: **www.hesperuspress.com**

ET REMOTISSIMA PROPE

SELECTED TITLES FROM HESPERUS PRESS